PRAISE FOR THE ANAÏS BLUE SERIES

The writing is, as usual from P.J. Whittlesea, flawless. Each character has their own flair, so perfectly captured on paper that they are almost tangible beings. I am enamoured of this this series, and can not wait for more.

— GOODREADS REVIEWER BELLE

This series is so unique and entertaining. I particularly enjoy the wisdom the author passes along to us as Anais deals with shades (ghosts) of well known celebrities. You won't believe which ones show up in this story. Great fun!

— GOODREADS REVIEWER MARGARET

I love the world building in this series. It's a refreshing change to all the 'same same' urban fantasies.

— GOODREADS REVIEWER LISA

OTHER BOOKS IN THE SERIES

The City of Shades: Anaïs Blue Prequel
Thistle Witch: Anaïs Blue Book 1
Discovering Magic: Anaïs Blue Book 2
A New Source of Magic: Anaïs Blue Book 3
A Witch's Calling: Anaïs Blue Book 4
Magic Awakes: Anaïs Blue Book 5

Visit **www.pjwhittlesea.com** for updates on releases.

A WITCH'S CALLING

ANAÏS BLUE BOOK FOUR

P J WHITTLESEA

tyet

First edition

A catalogue record of this book is available from the Royal Dutch National Library (Koninklijke Bibliotheek).

Published by Tyet Books, Amsterdam

www.tyetbooks.com

information@tyetbooks.com

ISBN 9789492523280

Cover Design by Miblart

Edited by Philip Newey

For Maurice, Lyn, Mary, and Margaret.
Thanks for sticking with me. You rock!

Life is not measured by the number of breaths we take, but by the moments that take our breath away.

— MAYA ANGELOU 1928–2014

CHAOS

In the beginning there was peace. There was calm in the world. At least this was the case on the preternatural side. Witches had their act together. Naturals, however, did not.

Regrettably they were, and still are, incapable of peace. They do not have a fully formed knowledge of the universe. This throws everything into disarray. This lack of knowledge, this insecurity in their perceived future, reduces them to petty infighting and squabbles about the most unimportant things.

Who really cares about the colour of another's skin? Why be bothered by what someone else believes? What makes one culture better than another?

What is it that drives this fight for inequality, when, at the dawn of time, all were declared equal? It's the most unnatural thing. But then, mankind is the exception to the rule in terms of life on this planet. Man is a freak of nature.

At his heart man is an individual. One with

individual thoughts and ideals. One with the will to protect them. Cohabitation goes against his instinct. Not unlike witches, naturals perform better in isolation where they don't get on each other's nerves. Unfortunately, being alone all the time is no party. Just ask a witch.

We all have a control centre which requires the occasional outlet—a brain which is far too busy. It invents stuff—lots of it—and all the time. Burdened with a continual process of ceaseless mental activity, it needs regular purging to function efficiently.

The cerebrum suffers from overkill. Urged on by the brain's insatiable activity, everything humanity does leads to the same result: wastage.

Also, for some reason, things of no intrinsic value, and of no use whatsoever, are considered worth more than anything which actually has a practical use. Like the magpie, mankind is drawn to shiny objects. In modern times it has even been given a name: bling. However, even this is not strictly true. The magpie has been falsely accused of its fixation with all things glittering. It's yet another example of naturals fobbing the blame off onto someone else. Why does a worthless bit of metal or crystal buried deep under the ground drive men to murder? Naturals often become too easily obsessed with face value. Perhaps it's the by-product of an overactive brain.

For the longest of times, witches were immune to these very human failings. Then they lost it. Even they are prone to losing complete control over their brains. Although, admittedly, they are able to put them to better use. One thing in particular led to their downfall: jealousy.

This emotion draws on the same base desire for shiny objects. Witch or non-witch, we often want what we can't possibly have. If we let our desires control us, then it all turns pear-shaped.

In the case of witchdom, it upset the entire balance of the universe. Jealousy turned something which was beautiful, harmonious and peaceful into chaos. And once chaos snags a foothold, it spreads like a disease. The virus took hold, prevailed, and practically destroyed everything in its wake.

The immediate reaction was to hope that, by ignoring it, chaos would go away. Ignorance, however, is rarely an advisable course of action. Allowing anything toxic to fester and grow only feeds it. Unfortunately, that is the way of the world.

Nature itself is a sort of organised chaos. Thankfully, a more positive one. It will reclaim all when left to its own devices. Stray pieces of litter, houses and even cities which have been abandoned are eventually swallowed up by the power of nature. It is an unstoppable force.

There is much talk of environmental damage to the planet and ways in which naturals should counteract the declining health of the Earth. The answer is pure and simple: stop. Do nothing. Accept it: nature cannot be tamed or controlled. Stop kidding yourself, as mere mortals, that you have any control over it whatsoever. Let it do its thing. Allow it some breathing space. Stand back and give it room. When given the chance, it will come back with a vengeance.

Chaos, however, cannot be completely ignored. It cannot be controlled by doing absolutely nothing. It must be actively treated. But with great care. In much the same way as with nature, naturals feel they must intervene. They can't help themselves. This intervention only aggravates chaos. This causes it to thrive. It loves being poked and prodded. Chaos should never be toyed with.

If you are aware of this, you can bring it to a halt. Handle it with oven gloves. Don't touch it. Contain it and bottle it away. If contained, chaos harms nobody. It will only harm itself, and, in doing so, eventually self-destruct.

The chaos which reigned in the witch community was relatively contained, but in no way controlled. The rift which ran through it was a fathomless wound. One which had been permitted to grow and fester over decades. In order to kill it, it was necessary to find out what fed it. And without knowing the whole story, it was very difficult to uncover the source of its nourishment.

Anaïs was the most recent addition to a line which stretched back for eons. As a novice, she was the key to everything. Her ignorance could take her places no one else could go. Purely because she wasn't blinded by facts. She was not suffering from information overload. Or jealousy. Her brain had space. She was a half-full vessel keen to be filled. But if filled the wrong way, she would only exacerbate the problem.

And chaos loves problems.

DOWN THE MOUNTAIN

The promptuary guided them into a tunnel on the far side of the lake. The boat zipped through it at high speed. The tunnel was narrower than the one they had taken to get up the mountain. Displaced water slewed up the rounded walls.

Sitting in silence, Anaïs closed her eyes. For a long time, she listened to the sound of the water and let the gentle swaying of the boat rock her from side to side. She cleared her head, forcing it blank, not wanting to recall what had happened in the volcano's crater. Nor the trials and tribulations of the days before.

A loud crash sounded behind her.

She opened her eyes, arched her neck and looked over the stern. The tunnel had narrowed further. The crash was caused by the sheets of water thrown up in their wake, smashing together. What was essentially a wall of water obscured everything. If they were being followed, it would be impossible for them to be seen or overrun.

The cacophony of rushing water grew, the sound tremendous, making any form of communication impossible.

Anaïs turned her attention to the front of the boat. She watched Ella struggle to keep the craft centred in the tunnel. Joan, in her body-builder guise, still had her sights set firmly on the windscreen. Like a rag doll, her head lolled around on her thick neck, moving easily with the movement of the boat.

Seated next to Anaïs, Nan prodded the little witch in the ribs with her elbow. *'Who's that?'*

Anaïs glanced sideways at the shade. Engrossed in her own preoccupations, she had completely forgotten about her caretaker. 'One moment, Nan.' Anaïs rummaged in her beret and pulled out her sunglasses. She slipped them on. Nan's camouflage dropped, revealing her true physical self. Anaïs smiled. It was good to have her back. 'Sorry.' She pointed at the sunglasses. 'You look better this way.'

Nan beamed. *'Good!'* She flicked her thumb towards the bow of the boat. *'Who's that?'*

'Which one?'

'The driver.'

'Oh, that's Ella.'

Nan cocked her head. *'Ella?'*

'Yeah,' said Anaïs. 'She's another Apothecary. You know, like Hank.'

'Hank?'

Anaïs furrowed her brow. 'Don't you remember him? You know, the Apothecary from Amsterdam. We met him in Barcelona as well.'

'Oh yes, I remember him. But it's vague. I can only recall snippets.' Partially defeated by her predicament, her shoulders slumped. *'I think I'm losing my memory. Stuff is fading.'*

'Then we'll have to do something about that,' said Anaïs with concern. She recalled Elvis and how his memories had faded completely. 'It's a definite shade problem.'

'It will definitely become a problem if it continues.'

'Then we'll have to work fast.'

Nan paused. They sat in silence for a moment.

Anaïs heard her sigh. She changed the subject. 'Supposedly, Hank and Ella were an item.'

The caretaker stared at the Apothecary. *'They were an item? I honestly can't picture her and Hank.'*

Anaïs grinned. 'You're not alone there.'

'And the other one?' Nan tilted her head towards Joan.

Anaïs cracked a mischievous grin. 'Oh, her!'

'Her? It's a guy. And very much one if you ask me. Bit of a workout junkie by the looks of it.'

Anaïs shook her head emphatically. 'No, it's not a guy. That's just her disguise—her camouflage. It's most certainly a girl—kind of a famous one.'

Nan straightened in her seat. *'Really? Who is it then?'*

Anaïs paused for effect, then spoke with deliberation. 'Joan of Arc.'

Nan's eyes widened. *'Joan of Arc?'*

'Yep.'

'Wow!'

Anaïs grinned. 'That's what I thought too.'

'What else have I missed?'

'Loads of stuff. To be honest, I'm not quite sure where to begin.' Anaïs played with the beading on the seat between them.

'Just tell me what you know. Maybe then we can piece it all together.'

'Maybe,' said Anaïs, pondering where to begin. 'What about the Inquisitor? Did you talk to him?'

'No, he said nothing to me.'

'Strange.' She studied the caretaker's face. 'I had an interesting time while you were with him.'

'I can imagine. What happened?'

'I met your father.'

Nan frowned. *'My father?'*

Anaïs nodded grimly. 'It turns out—that is, if I'm to believe him—that he is also my father.'

'What? Really?' Nan puffed her cheeks. *'But that makes us …'*

'Sisters. Well, half-sisters. Thankfully Caput Mortuum is not my mother.'

'Wow!' Nan dropped her gaze to the back of the seat before her.

'Do you know him?'

'My father?' Nan shook her head. *'No, we never met, and my mother refused to talk about him.'*

'You'll never guess his name.'

'Oh, that I know.'

'Really?' Anaïs raised an eyebrow.

'Deus Dominus. Is he as pompous as his name?'

Anaïs chuckled. 'Yep, even more so.'

Nan flashed a grin before a serious expression

clouded her face. She pursed her lips and shook her head. *'What a family. I can't believe we are sisters.'*

'Me either.' Anaïs reached over and took Nan's hand. She squeezed it, then quickly released it. It was bitterly cold. She rubbed warmth back into her palm. She assessed Nan's face. 'I think it's kind of cool we're sisters. If what he said is on the level, that is. And there's more.' She took a deep breath and released it. 'I'm not sure I believe this either, but he said we are all related. According to him, the Inquisitor is your brother.'

Nan was speechless. She took a few moments to process this new information. *'But if we are siblings, why the hell did he do what he did with me?'*

Anaïs hunched her shoulders. 'No idea. Maybe he doesn't know who you are. There are so many secrets floating around, I doubt anyone knows the whole truth. Honestly, I don't know who to trust any more. The more I learn, the more confusing it all becomes.'

'Yes, it's complicated. I think the best course of action is to trust no one, Anaïs.'

'You're right. But I have to trust someone.'

'I'm here for you, Anaïs.'

'I know,' said the little witch. 'Apart from the obvious, there's another reason I was so desperate to get you back. Our father said he was trying to solve your problem. I don't believe him. I can't leave your wellbeing up to him. You're the only one I truly trust.'

'Good to know. I trust you too. Together we will solve this.' Nan sighed and slumped in her seat. She tilted her head back and rolled her eyes. *'Man! What a mess!'*

Sudden bright light blinded both of them. Anaïs squinted, shielding her eyes with her hand. The roof of the tunnel had disappeared.

THE CHASM

What had practically been a manmade construction, a lava tube filled with water, now became an irregular act of nature in an instant. The tunnel they had been travelling in transformed into a narrow causeway, flanked on both sides by high cliffs. They were in a deep chasm. The light which had blinded Anaïs was the sun's dawn rays streaming along it.

Glancing over her shoulder, Anaïs saw more tunnels feeding into the chasm. Under high pressure, the combined streams of water gushed up the walls of the cliffs. It showered them with spray. A particularly large wave hit an outcrop high in the cliff wall. It arced over them before crashing down on the boat, saturating them.

Anaïs wiped water from her face with the palm of her hand and shivered involuntarily. She glanced at the Apothecary. Ella's brow was furrowed deeply. In full concentration, her eyes focussed on the path ahead, the Apothecary bit her bottom lip.

The relatively smooth sides of the chasm became less so. Great boulders jutted out from the rocky walls. Although the waterway widened, the course along it was far from straightforward. It became an obstacle course. Rocks which had fallen into the stream created islands of destruction which had to be avoided at all costs.

Anaïs sucked in her breath. She eyed the speedboat's chrome-plated hull. *How strong is this thing?* Glancing up, she watched the Apothecary's erratic movements. *Can Ella even cope with this?*

The Apothecary tightened her grip on the Dreadnought's wheel, her knuckles whitening. She wrenched the wheel from left to right, fighting to carve a course between the rocks. No longer a barrel-straight path which was relatively simple to negotiate, the river became a rapid-impeded causeway with tight curves and blind corners.

One such corner loomed before them. A sheer cliff wall—a dead end. Ella grabbed the accelerator lever and snapped it back towards her, throwing the craft into reverse. The motor roared. Behind Anaïs, the bristling pipes of the craft's exhaust manifold spat out a massive plume of black smoke. The Dreadnought slowed, but not nearly enough to prevent them from being smashed to splinters if they collided with the rock face. Nothing could compete with the strong current which now pushed them down the mountain. The water flow was a force unto itself.

Anaïs threw up her arms, crossing them in front of her face and steeling herself for impact. Out of the corner of her eye, she saw the continuation of the river. They were approaching a ninety-degree kink. Ella saw it too.

The Apothecary whipped the wheel to the right into a full lock position. The craft slewed sideways. Ploughing through the water it pushed a wave before it. This served as a buffer, preventing the vessel from dashing itself on the unyielding wall before them. Moments before contact, Ella drove her hand down hard on the accelerator, snapping it forward on the console and powering the boat towards the continuation of the river. As they barrelled alongside it, the hull made the slightest contact with the cliff face, emitting a tiny squeak as it did.

The terror of what had already been a scary ride increased exponentially. The river narrowed and widened without warning. The depth varied unpredictably too. At times, the hull bottomed out on rocks on the river bed, producing an ear-splitting screech. Drop-offs fell away beneath them, causing the craft to become airborne. They soared through the air after being launched from a medium-sized waterfall. Their flight was momentary as the boat swiftly responded to gravity. The impact as they crashed back down on the water's hard surface took the wind out of Anaïs.

Sudden changes in the course of the river kept Ella constantly twitching from side to side in her seat. Anaïs watched her use her entire body to guide the craft. Occasionally, the channel suddenly forked, forcing Ella to make split-second decisions as to which way to go.

Where are we?

The promptuary had slipped onto the floor. Unable to reach it, and not daring to let go of her grip on the edge of her seat, Anaïs decided to forget about their destination. Survival was their primary concern.

This has to end somewhere!

As if on command, the waterway obliged.

The stone cliffs dropped in elevation. A thick line of trees replaced the stone walls. They hung over the causeway, creating a tunnel of foliage. The sudden overgrowth obscured her view of the path ahead. She felt the boat became airborne once more. They soared through the branches of the overhanging trees. Miraculously, they avoided hitting any of them.

In a flurry of leaves, snapping twigs and spray, they dropped several metres into a pond of surprisingly still water. The craft was brought to an almost instantaneous halt. As the nose of the Dreadnought ploughed into the pond, a great wave cascaded over the bow, soaking them all once again. Thrown forward, Anaïs slid from her seat to the floor, jarring her face on the rear of the front seat.

Ella, the only occupant not thrown forward due to her grip on the steering wheel, arched her spine over the backrest. She flexed her jarred wrists and slumped forward over the steering wheel. 'I think I'm going to need a moment,' she murmured.

'No problem. I think we all do,' said Anaïs as she climbed back onto her seat. She massaged her nose, which had taken the full brunt of the collision. Gingerly, she bent it from side to side, checking it was not broken. Satisfied no permanent damage had been done, she breathed a sigh of relief. She eyed the others.

'Take all the time you need,' she said.

THE CAVE

Ella had recovered from her exhausting ordeal and guided the boat slowly across the small patch of water. Above it, a canopy of trees blocked out the sky. At one end of the little lake was a sheer cliff face. Hidden in the folds of rock, they discovered a narrow crevice. As they motored down it, the walls and ceiling closed in, forming another tunnel. Once again, they were plunged into darkness.

Joan performed her trick of illumination. The light from the shade exposed the interior. Unlike the narrow tunnels they had previously experienced, they were now in a cave of generous proportions. Above them hung a forest of stalactites. Their sharp points hung menacingly over their heads. Hanging from the ceiling was a large colony of bats.

The pungent odour of bat guano permeated Anaïs's nostrils. She scrunched up her nose. Retrieving it from the floor of the boat, she consulted her promptuary.

'Show me where we are,' Anaïs commanded the handbook.

As before, a holographic three-dimensional impression of the island materialised above the open pages. A purple star appeared, and the book homed in on it. As it zoomed in Anaïs caught a glimpse of the outline of Mount Etna and the congested streets of Catania. They were near a coastal town somewhere to the north of the city.

'Where are we exactly?' enquired Anaïs.

The map faded and a single word appeared on the open pages: TAORMINA.

'And where is Immi?'

The letters faded, and the map reappeared. The promptuary zoomed out. A dot appeared to accompany the star representing their own position. The librarian was still in the city of Catania.

'We're still on the right track,' said Anaïs. 'Keep going, Ella.' She closed the handbook and shoved it in her coat pocket.

As they continued along the waterway, the cave became more congested. Stalactites joined stalagmites, forming thick trees of limestone. With the motorboat's engine set to idle, Ella threaded her way between the trunks of the petrified forest. The soft sound of the motor purring was virtually drowned out by the noise of constant dripping.

Anaïs had the feeling they were travelling down into the bowels of the Earth. Almost like being in the womb of a mother. The appearance of their surrounds was not dissimilar to the internals of a life form under a microscope. The rivulets of water running down the trunks looked like veins and arteries. They glistened in blue and red.

Joan let out a gasp and extinguished her light. *'Désolé. Sorry,'* she panted, trying to catch her breath.

Anaïs patted her on the shoulder, then quickly retracted her hand. The icy contact was more intense than ever. 'It's okay, Joan. I understand.' Her eyes swiftly adjusted to the lack of light.

'Wow!' Nan and the Apothecary gasped in unison. The stereo effect of the internal and external voices caused the little witch to screw up her face in disconcertion.

Anaïs joined them in surveying the cave. To her surprise the cavern supplied its own source of illumination. Millions of tiny pinpoints of light surrounded them, winking like stars in the night sky and reflecting off the water beneath them. It was as if they floated in space.

'I must say,' said Ella, breaking the silence, 'you may be able to practise magic, Anaïs, but nothing beats nature's magic.'

Anaïs smiled. 'You're not kidding there, Ella.'

They exited the forest of limestone trunks. The cavern narrowed. A ledge formed on one side, jutting out from the cave wall. Eventually, the waterway tapered to a point where they could go no further.

'End of the line,' said Ella matter-of-factly.

They clambered out of the boat. With Anaïs leading the small party, they shuffled single-file along the ledge. It led to a corridor hewn from solid rock.

Feeling around in the darkness, Anaïs ran her hands along the walls of the corridor. Its smooth sides were wet to the touch. Underfoot, Anaïs heard swishing as she slid her boots through a layer of water. The darkness was short-lived. As they moved onwards, thin shafts of light streamed from above through cracks in the rock, illuminating their way until it was barred by an oak door. The dark wood was rotten, apart from an emblem embedded into its surface. In contrast to the door, it was impervious to decay. Gleaming in gold was a brass star.

Anaïs ran her finger over its contours. She smirked. 'Looks like we're in the right place.'

'Yes,' said Ella. 'This island is certainly full of surprises.'

'I've gotten used to them,' said Anaïs.

'Well, what are we waiting for then?' Ella nudged the witch. 'Open the door.'

'Getting used to surprises doesn't mean I like them. Who knows what's on the other side.'

Ella hunched her shoulders. 'We can't stay here.'

'You're right.' Anaïs cranked the handle and pushed. The door did not yield. She set her weight against it. Still, it would not budge.

'Maybe you need to pull it?'

Anaïs scratched her head. 'Maybe.' She turned the handle and pulled on the door. It opened easily.

'Sometimes the solution is simpler than you think,' said Ella, chuckling.

Anaïs grinned. 'Yes, you're right. I'll make a mental note not to overthink things in the future.'

Ella laughed. ‘There’s not much to overthink with a door.’

Anaïs shook her head. ‘No, I guess there isn’t. Shall we?’

‘After you,’ said Ella with a sweep of her hand.

They filed through the doorway. The corridor continued. As they moved down it, Anaïs noted slots carved into the walls. Most were empty. Some held oblong boxes; others contained the torn remnants of cloth.

The further they went the more apparent it became exactly what the slots were for. Some of them contained corpses. They were in an underground burial chamber. Wrapped in shrouds, many seemed relatively well-preserved considering the damp conditions, appearing as if they had only recently been laid to rest.

‘This place is creepy,’ said Ella.

‘You’re telling me,’ replied the witch.

As they continued through the tomb a movement caught Anaïs’s eye. In one of the slots a burial shroud seemed to flap. Was it a breeze? She stopped and peered closely at the contents of the slot. She caught her breath.

The mummified remains of a young woman rolled towards her. Her face exposed, she opened her eyes. The look chilled Anaïs to the bone.

She choked on her breath before recovering. Avoiding the gaze of the mummy, she hissed at the others, ‘Let’s get out of here. Now!’

ENTOMBED

Anaïs led the way. She ran down the corridor with the rest in tow. The movement in the burial slots became frantic. The mummified dead tossed and turned in their beds. Some of them flung their arms out as Anaïs passed them by. She weaved, ducked and dodged to avoid them. But, even so, occasionally they made contact. The sharp, icy chill of thin fingers dragging over her arm shot through her entire body. This was a chill far stronger than what she had previously experienced with her shades. It froze her to the core.

She heard a yelp from behind her. She turned to see Ella caught in the clutches of a mummy. Anaïs ran back to her and brought her own arm down hard on the offending limb. The arm, more bone than flesh, dislocated from its owner's shoulder. Hitting the stone floor, it clattered like dice dropping on a slate table.

Her eyes glazed over, frozen and rooted to the spot, the Apothecary's entire body shook, shivering uncontrollably. Anaïs punched her on the bicep to snap her out of her daze. 'Ella!' she yelled at her.

The Apothecary's pale complexion glowed in the dim light. She blinked and stared blankly at Anaïs. The little witch waved her hand in front of the Apothecary's face. She snapped her fingers. 'Ella! Look at me!' She pointed at her own eyes, indicating to Ella that she should look into them. 'Move!'

Ella's half-hypnotic state faded. She nodded firmly. 'Okay.'

Squeezing past Anaïs, she continued down the corridor. Behind them the shades followed. The mummies paid no attention to them, even retracting back into their slots as they moved along the corridor. Clearly, the dead were only interested in the living. *Strange.*

Anaïs felt something grappling at her foot. Looking down she saw the rotten fingers of the dislocated arm clawing at the toe of her boot. She shrank back in horror before gathering herself. *Don't be such a wuss! Pull yourself together!*

She swung back a leg, took aim, and kicked the limb down the corridor past the shades. Joan and Nan dodged it. They pulled up beside her. *Maybe keeping them close is better. At least they have some kind of defence.* She cocked her head towards the Apothecary disappearing down the corridor. 'Let's keep going. Follow Ella.'

Anaïs did not wait for a reply. She spun on her heels. Next to her a mummy sat bolt-upright in its slot. It was very small. The shroud fell from its head exposing its face—the decomposing face of a small child. Anaïs gulped. The child opened its eyes. Eyes which were clear and bright, and seemingly very much alive. Filled with a mixture of pain and fear, they cut straight through the little witch.

Anaïs was mesmerised.

She felt drawn into the eyes. The rest of the room faded into mist. Anaïs saw only the eyes. Two penetrating orbs floating in black space. She no longer heard a sound—the constant drip of water faded to nothingness, replaced with a deafening silence.

An invisible force drew her closer. Anaïs fought the pull to no avail. It was far too strong. Involuntarily, she slid her foot across the floor. She took a step towards the child. Images filled her head: fire; explosions; a sea of wooden splinters and chips of rock flying through the air. Untold destruction prevailed. Anaïs stood at its very centre.

A noise broke the silence—a low howl rapidly turned into a long-drawn-out scream. A feeling of intense fear overcame her. The fear was not her own. It came from the child. She began to perspire. The sweat on her brow formed instantaneously. She felt its wetness under her collar. She had the oddest, unmistakable urge to strip off all her clothing. Panic set in.

Get me out of here!

The hot flush disappeared. It was replaced by an extreme chill, and her head felt as if it would burst. Her vision became obscured. She saw a flurry of snow, or was it a blizzard?—perhaps static on a television? A random thought wandered through her brain. *What was the analogy to describe that again? A polar bear in a snow storm?*

A fresh spike of freezing pain shot through her skull, cutting off the thought. 'Ow!'

The calm, reassuring voice of her caretaker cut through the haze. *'Anaïs? Are you all right?'*

Anaïs closed her eyes—hard—screwing them into tiny balls. She tried to shake her head to clear it. She could not move it. She snapped her eyes open. Nan's face swam into view, her hand upon the witch's head. Anaïs brushed it away. She grasped her skull.

'Ow!' she cried again.

'What?' enquired Nan.

'Brain freeze.'

'Oops! Sorry about that.'

'No problem, Nan,' said Anaïs, massaging her head through her beret. 'It worked.'

'You were totally out there. What happened?'

'It happened.' Anaïs nodded at the mummified child. She glanced sideways at it, not daring to look it in the eye. The child sat in the same position, staring at her. It appeared to be in a trance as much as Anaïs had been. The little witch averted her eyes. She cleared her throat loudly. 'Freaky stuff.'

She reassured herself. *Maybe being a wuss is not such a bad thing.* She surveyed the corridor. A mummy stirred in every available slot. Strangely, even those which had previously been empty. *What the heck is going on here? Shades don't do this.* She glanced at Nan. 'Let's get out of here quick. This place is creeping me out.'

Cupping her hands around her eye sockets to avoid looking at the mummies, she set off down the corridor.

She called out to the Apothecary, 'Ella! Are you still there?'

Anaïs heard her distant call. She continued towards it. Ella responded again, her voice louder now. 'I think I've found a way out.'

Between panting for breath, Anaïs managed a sigh. *Thank goodness!*

THE EYES HAVE IT

Eyes are a dead giveaway. You can't hide behind them, even if you exist in another realm. The eye is also supposedly the gateway to the soul. In the case of shades it is the only part of their true appearance that their camouflage does not hide.

Shades often give naturals 'the eye' but most don't respond. People rarely look deeply into each other's eyes unless they want something themselves.

Eye contact is the basis of all direct connections. It can convey all kinds of things: from love to boredom to rage. It is the only infallible way to tell if someone is really paying attention. The dead are no exception.

They are constantly on the lookout for someone or something which will respond to them. However, fixing someone with a penetrating stare is usually pointless. It drives them away. People will just think you're strange. And staring is impolite.

Under most circumstances, having your eyes exposed is of no benefit at all. People cannot read thoughts anyway. Unless, of course, they have had a certain degree of witch training. And, as in the case with shade camouflage, without any added facial expression the message will invariably get lost.

If you were able to look deeply enough you might be surprised to see more than you expected. The ability to look deeply into the soul generally only comes as a witch progresses in age. It also correlates directly with a witch's worldliness. Experience is crucial to gaining a correct reading.

Age itself doesn't automatically bring more useful knowledge. Children can make better use of their knowledge. They have less of it to cloud their judgement. They are more open. They make interpretations based on face value. Once older you tend to be weighed down with an overkill of experience and quite often can't connect the right piece of knowhow with your present predicament. It can get very confusing.

Unfortunately, the young are also under the misconception they know more than they do. This can be a disadvantage. Signals obvious to those of age can easily be lost or misconstrued by the young. What one age group has, the other has not. There is no perfect balance. Let's just conclude there is no advantage to being from either party.

If the living have problems, spare a thought for shades. Being dead has very few advantages. The lack of any proper communication will get you nowhere. Naturally this is incredibly frustrating. This does not, however, stop shades from trying. What else are you going to do with your time?

Under usual circumstances, naturals remain oblivious to a shade's cries for attention. They can flash their eyes all they like. Naturals will just think it's weird and look the other way. Or, in a worst case scenario, run the other way.

Unfortunately, for a witch, avoiding a penetrating stare is not as simple. Escape requires more than ignoring. Especially when they are fully aware of what they are dealing with. It is their task to help the dead. But not every case can be dealt with all at once. Shades have to get in line. And it's a long queue.

As a novice, Anaïs had not experienced the stare lock before. It can be a dangerous thing, akin to the mesmerising glare of an animal predator about to seize its prey. If you are unable to escape it, you may be lost forever. You will become dinner.

Shades have this predatory instinct, but it is not fully honed. Although, in the case of the child in the tomb, its innocence worked to its advantage. Thankfully for Anaïs, a rescue had been forthcoming.

For one little witch it would serve as warning. You may get close to a shade, but too close is not always advisable. As with Anaïs, it can scare you senseless.

SURFACING

With Nan and Joan on her heels, Anaïs rushed around a slight kink in the corridor, only to be met with its abrupt end. She slid to a halt, practically colliding with the Apothecary. The shades almost did the same with Anaïs. They avoided the witch but collided with each other before coming to a stop.

Ella barely acknowledged their presence, her full attention directed towards the door which stood before her. It sealed the end of the corridor. Having taken a short break to muster her strength, she resumed wrestling with it. The door remained uncooperative. It refused to yield.

Anaïs shuffled on the spot impatiently. 'What's the problem?'

'It's stuck.'

The little witch glanced back at the section of corridor behind her. To her relief there were no tombs in the section leading up to the door.

'Maybe you're trying to open it the wrong way,' Anaïs postulated. 'You know, like I did before.'

'No, that's not it. It opens outwards. There has to be something jammed against it.' Ella tried to make light of the situation. She grinned and winked at Anaïs. 'There's never a battering ram around when you need one.'

Behind them, out of sight round the bend in the corridor, the sound of movement grew louder. A frigid breeze carried the sound to them. It ruffled Anaïs's hair. The fine follicles on her neck stood on end. She shivered involuntarily.

What are they doing? Getting out of their tombs? Surely not. Not looking like that. In their true physical form. There are rules in place to stop that. She glanced at the door barring their escape route. *Whatever! No time for this. Ignore them! Just get the hell out of here!*

Anaïs tried to compose herself, but the shivering became uncontrollable. 'Brrr … it's so cold,' she said through chattering teeth. She rubbed her arms in an effort to work some warmth into them. It staved off the cold long enough for her to appraise the door properly.

The Apothecary grabbed the door handle and braced herself for another attempt.

'Hold on, Ella,' said Anaïs, 'let me give it a go.' She rummaged around in her beret. She frowned. 'I'm sure it's here somewhere.' She thrust her arm deeper, all the way up to her shoulder.

Ella watched the arm disappear. She smirked and shook her head. 'I can't get over how cool that is. Although, how you ever find what you're looking for in there is a mystery to me. Surely there must be a better way of storing stuff.'

Anaïs paused and shrugged. 'I'm sure there is, but it's all I've got.' Resuming her search she touched something cold, wet and sticky. She screwed up her face. 'Eeuw!'

Ella's eyes widened. 'What?'

Realising what she had found, the little witch expelled a puff of air, her frosted breath producing a vapour cloud. 'It's okay, Ella. Nothing to be concerned about. I think I just found that piece of pizza I was storing for safe keeping.'

'Probably a good idea to get rid of it,' said Ella, who had now joined Anaïs in shivering from the chilly breeze. 'We're in Italy after all. You can always get a new slice.'

Anaïs nodded. 'You have a good point there.' She withdrew her hand. In it was an unidentifiable white and red glob. She shook her hand, releasing the sticky substance. It hit the floor with a wet slap. She wiped her hand on her coat, leaving behind a tacky streak.

'Anaïs, please!'

The witch dropped her chin. 'Sorry, Nan.'

Ella glanced at the shade's blank face, confused as to why Anaïs had cause to apologise. An increase in the noise down the corridor drew her attention. She looked earnestly over Nan's shoulder. 'No pressure, Anaïs,' said Ella hastily, 'but I think we *really* need to hurry.'

'Yes, yes. You're right.' Anaïs reached back into the beret. Concentrating, she visualised what she was looking for. A slender pencil-like object jumped into her hand. Her eyes lit up. 'Got it!'

Anaïs pulled the object out of the beret. She replaced the hat on her head and held up her hand. In it was a multi-coloured child's windmill.

'What's that?' enquired Ella.

'Oh, it's something I picked up in Amsterdam,' said Anaïs with glee. 'It came in really useful in Barcelona. I think it might do the job here.'

Ella furrowed her brow. 'I don't see how.'

'Tell her, Nan.' She glanced from the shade to Ella. 'Oh, sorry, you can't.' She waved the others behind her. 'You all better stand back.'

Ella and the shades did as instructed, giving the little witch some space. Anaïs widened her stance and gripped the windmill with both hands. She pointed it towards the door and blew softly on the blades. Slowly, they began to turn.

She focussed on the door. Closing her eyes, she kept an image of it in her mind's eye. A sudden bright flash of light cleared her vision. It flushed all thoughts from her brain, sending it blank. Behind her lids she saw only a white slate.

Within moments her subliminal vision returned. Shapes appeared. They swam before her and began to configure themselves into an identifiable form. She recognised it as the grains of wood. She was in the door itself. Buried deep in the timber, she could see its structure, the fine lines of its growth rings, its knots and cracks. She could even smell it—the sweet odour of sap.

There were pockets of empty space. Using her mind, she dived into one of them. It was a tunnel.

What is it with all the tunnels? I've barely been out of one since I left Malta. Mentally, she slapped herself. *Enough! Pull yourself together! Concentrate! Keep going!*

The tunnel snaked its way through the wood. Sweeping around a corner she came face to face with an insect. A termite. She drew in her breath sharply. It filled the tunnel. Its head was huge. In fact, everything about it was huge. Its giant eyes with all their tiny lenses glinted at her. Its antennae swept over her head like the branches of some enormous tree. Its razor-edged mandibles opened.

Forget going forward! Just get me out of here!

She flew backwards, leaving the insect behind and retracing her journey along the tunnel. Then she was out of it. Back in solid timber. The microscopic view shrank. The details of the wood lessened. The last she glimpsed of its structure was that it was riddled with termites. The door's seemingly solid exterior was a fragile exoskeleton.

Wow! That was weird. So now I can teleport or something?

Anaïs opened her eyes. As she did her hearing returned, taking her by surprise. Her entire time in the confines of the wooden door had been in silence. The windmill in her hands emitted a ceaseless high-pitched screech. The blades moved so fast they glowed, a hot ring of light surrounding them. She could feel the heat they generated.

Curiously, Anaïs felt no wind. It was as if she stood

in the eye of the storm. She glanced to one side. Ella was certainly not in the calm eye. Flattened against the wall, she was buffeted by the fierce wind coming from the toy in the witch's hands. The skin on her face was contorted. Her cheeks rippled, the skin undulating like ocean waves, as if she were suffering the effects of riding in a high-gravity centrifuge, spinning at a high rate of knots.

Oops! Better do this quick! thought Anaïs. She concentrated on the windmill in her hands. She urged it on. Glancing over its fiery halo she peered at the door. Nothing seemed to be happening. *Damn! It's not working!* She peered more closely at the door's surface. *Wait … it is!*

What was left of a thin layer of paint coating the wood began to slowly dislodge. The wind pried tiny flakes of it free. The peeled edges of larger strips held vainly onto the surface. They flapped in the wind before losing their grip on the woodwork. They flew outwards. The flakes spread themselves across the wall and ceiling around the door, coating them with a new finish.

From the exposed timber, small splinters of wood stood on end like spines on a porcupine. They too dislodged themselves and began to fly off. Larger chunks of wood followed. Holes formed in the door's surface.

The door held its structure briefly, resisting the power of the windmill. Then it succumbed. It disintegrated into a cloud of sawdust. Anaïs released her grip on the windmill. Inert and no longer spinning, the toy fell to the floor. As it did, the wind died.

Clinging to the wall beside Anaïs, Ella released her grip. She slid to the floor, the exposed skin on her arms squeaking on the smooth, marble-like stone surface. She cringed and massaged her forearms. Although gasping for air, she managed to regulate her breathing enough to expel a stream of expletives.

Anaïs reddened.

Ella drew in a lungful of air. Then expelled it. Calming herself, she murmured, 'You might have warned me about the gale-force winds.'

'Sorry,' said Anaïs apologetically. 'It did its job, though. Didn't it?'

Nodding slowly in agreement, Ella warily eyed the toy on the floor.

They both turned their attention to the opening left by the obliterated door. Beyond the doorway the corridor continued. However, it was no longer a corridor. The ceiling had collapsed, filling it with rubble. The stone remnants of the ceiling, which had clearly created the barrier beyond the door, tumbled into the room. A thin ray of sunlight streaming through a crack above the rubble played over the mound of rocks.

Anaïs's joy at seeing the light was quickly dampened.

In tandem with the sunlight came a gust of fresh air. It did not remain fresh for long. On it floated the pungent odour of smoke.

Great! thought Anaïs. *Just what we need right now.*

SMOKE

Anaïs's nostrils twitched, the waft of smoke biting at them. She coughed and sighed.

'What is it?' enquired Ella.

Anaïs nodded towards the source of the sunlight. 'It's him.'

The Apothecary cocked her head. 'Him?'

'Don't you smell it?'

Ella inhaled deeply through her nostrils. She coughed and cleared her throat. 'Yes, a cigar. There's someone up there.' She brightened. 'Good. Maybe they can help us out.'

Anaïs shook her head vigorously. 'No, not good. We don't need that kind of help. He smokes them. The Inquisitor, the guy from the crater. The guy with the dogs. It's him up there somewhere.'

'Oh.' Ella paled. She lowered her voice. 'Are you sure?'

'I'd know that smell anywhere.'

'What do we do?'

Anaïs glanced over her shoulder. The sound of movement down the corridor continued to grow in volume. 'We can't stay here. We'll just have to face him.'

'Are you sure you want to do that?'

'No, Anaïs! Don't do it!'

The caretaker's voice barrelling through her head in tandem with Ella's threw Anaïs for a moment. She tapped the side of her skull with the soft of the palm of her hand. She glanced at Nan and then at Ella. 'I don't see that we have much choice in the matter.'

Anaïs bent down and scooped up the toy windmill.

'Besides,' she said, holding up the windmill. 'I have this. It worked on him in Barcelona. And then he still had a hellhound with him.' She creased her brow. Her voice firmed with determination. 'I don't expect it will be a walkover, but I've beaten him before. I can do it again.'

Ella studied the witch's face. 'You seem pretty sure of yourself.'

Anaïs's shoulders slumped. She stared at the floor and slowly shook her head. 'I'm not. To tell the truth, I'm shaking in my boots.' She straightened, lifted her head and grinned at Ella. 'But hey!' She threw her arms in the air. 'What's a witch to do?'

Ella frowned. 'It might be okay for you, but I'm no witch.'

'That's fine. I'm not asking for your help. You can just stay behind me.' Anaïs nudged the Apothecary with her elbow. 'Anyway, he's given himself away. We have the element of surprise.'

'I wouldn't be too sure about that,' said Ella

cautiously. 'If he knows we're here, it will be no surprise.'

Anaïs rubbed her chin thoughtfully. 'I don't think he knows precisely where we are. If at all. Otherwise he would be down here already. It's more important I know he's here. Usually I don't even have that.' She cracked a weak smile. 'That's enough for me.'

Anaïs turned to the shades. 'Nan, you and Joan keep an eye on her.' She nodded in Ella's direction. 'You better all keep behind me and out of sight until I've dealt with him.'

'Anaïs, maybe Ella's right.' Nan protested. *'Are you sure you want to do this?'*

'Yes.' Grimly she tightened her grip on the windmill. 'I'm sure.' She turned towards the doorway. Surveying the mound of rocks, she drew a deep breath and silently gathered her thoughts. *Let's deal with this sucker!*

Anaïs slipped the windmill into her coat pocket and began climbing the rockslide. The surface was loose. With each step she had to search for stable footing. She slipped and slid on the rocks. As she moved upwards the space between the rockslide and ceiling narrowed. She had to move stones aside in order to make enough room to squeeze through. The chink in the ceiling provided very little light. She had to rely on groping around to push the rubble aside. Occasionally she stopped and glanced behind her. Ella and the shades were a few metres below her at the foot of the rockslide.

Gradually, the mound of stones flattened out and the climb became easier. As she neared its source, the light grew in brightness. The strength of the pungent odour of cigar smoke grew with it. Doubt crept in. *He knows. He's up there waiting.* She rested for a moment and caught her breath. *No! Don't be an idiot. You can do this. Get it together.* She wiped the perspiration from her brow with her sleeve. She retrieved the windmill. Holding it up in front of her face, she drew reassurance from her weapon. *Yes, you can do this.* She spun its blades with her index finger.

She spoke softly. 'Are you ready, little guy?' The blades winked, reflecting the sunlight as they turned. *Okay! One last push!*

She took a final look behind her. Ella and the shades had begun to climb the rockslide. She motioned them to stop. 'Remember, stay out of sight,' she whispered hoarsely.

Ella nodded. Anaïs glanced from the Apothecary to the caretaker. She read concern in Nan's eyes but decided to ignore it. Nan would always be afraid for her. *Don't let that stop you. It's now or never!*

She turned her attention to the small opening above her. She crawled towards it. Without pausing she squeezed through the gap and out into broad daylight. On her knees, she squinted, shielding her eyes from the stark morning sun. *Oh, c'mon!* She willed her vision to adjust to the glare.

Peering out from under the shelter of her hand she could make out a figure silhouetted in the sunlight. It stood a few metres away. As her eyes adjusted she saw it was wearing a body-length cloak. A hood pulled low over its head covered its face.

The shrouded figure dropped the cigar it was

holding at its feet. It stamped on the butt, producing a shower of sparks. Twisting its boot, it ground the cigar deep into the dust and spoke. 'Hello, Miss Blue.'

The witch bit her lip. The voice was masculine, but it was not the Inquisitor's.

HIM AGAIN

Anaïs flared her nostrils. 'Thistle! My name is Anaïs Thistle!'

'I don't know you by that name,' said the figure gruffly. He raised his chin. His eyes shone, two pinpoints of light glowing in the shadows under his hood.

'Well, now you do,' she sneered.

Warily, Anaïs watched him as he tilted his head forward. He peeled back the hood, exposing the gleaming crown of his head to the light. It glinted menacingly. He raised his head and glared at her. She caught her breath. *Deus Dominus!* She choked on the air and rapidly expelled it. Slowly, she drew in another breath and mustered her strength.

'It's the one I've chosen for myself,' she said.

He cocked his head to one side. 'Why?'

His interest seemed genuine. Perhaps she could gain some time to think. She adopted a stronger stance. 'Blue is too common. To be perfectly honest, I hate it. I like purple.'

'Then why thistle?'

'It's a shade of purple.'

'Makes sense.' Deus rubbed the stubble on his chin. 'I guess.' He cleared his throat loudly. 'But we are not here to discuss your name.'

Anaïs eyed him intently, desperately trying to read his face. A blank canvas, it gave nothing away. 'No, I assume you're here to stop me.'

'I warned you before, Anaïs. You don't listen. You have done a terrible thing.' Deus glanced sideways up at Mount Etna towering above them. 'Where is your sister?'

Anaïs followed his gaze. Fed from the crater by a smouldering, dirty, grey stream, a pall of black smoke hung over the mountain. She frowned. She had sealed the volcano. Was it active again? Or was the smoke merely remnants of her magic? *Pay no attention to it. Deal with him!* She turned her attention to the Ethnarch.

She replied as innocently as she could. 'Sister?'

'Yes,' he nodded. 'You know, we spoke of her before. Your caretaker—Nan.'

She made a determined effort not to avert her eyes from his face. *Don't give anything away. Whatever you do, don't give them away. Aw heck! Maybe I've done it already. He better not be able to read minds.* She fought to keep her expression steady. Feeling herself faltering, she knotted her brow. 'She's safe.'

'She won't stay that way forever. Her time is limited.

She will fade. Only I can help her.' He clasped the lapels of his cloak. 'Where is she?'

'I told you, she's safe.'

'I don't have time for games, Anaïs,' he growled. 'Tell me.'

Anaïs formed a thin slit with her lips and spoke brusquely out of the corner of them, 'No.'

He straightened, drawing himself up to his full height. He looked down his nose at her. 'So be it,' he said grimly. 'We will do this another way.'

He released the grip on one lapel and reached deep into his cloak. From the folds he pulled the oldest book Anaïs had ever seen. Its cover was tattered and grubby. More a loose-leaf notebook than a bound volume, the ragged edges of the leaves of paper looked as if they had been stuffed between the covers. The only part of it which appeared to have avoided the rigours of age was a golden star. Embossed on the front cover, it glinted in the light in much the same way as the Ethnarch's shaven skull.

Anaïs glanced around her, taking in the lie of the land. They were in the ruins of what appeared to be an ancient fortress. Out in the bay, between other buildings, she could make out the turquoise waters of the Mediterranean. She edged sideways and peered over a low wall next to her. They were in the upper area of a town. The town itself, nestled on a hillside, fanned out below them. Along the coast and sprawling out in the distance was a large city. *That has to be Catania.*

Behind her was the entrance to the cave. In front he

barred the only escape route: a narrow, walled, stone escarpment leading down the hill.

'Last chance, Anaïs,' Deus said sternly. 'We can do this the easy way. You answer my question. Or we can do it the hard way. Either way you will tell me what I want to know.' He paused, puffing out his chest. 'What's it going to be? Your choice.'

Some choice! She dropped her eyes to avoid his stare. She looked at her hands. There it was, as it had been the entire time. The little toy windmill, lying across her fingers in her loose grip. How had she forgotten about it? *His talk, that's how. Stuff his choices. I have one of my own. A plan of attack. Simple. Easy. Lift and blow.*

Before she could move he stepped forward. Reaching out he placed his hand on her head. Immediately the star on the book clasped against his chest began to emit tiny blue arcs of electrical static. The arcs ran swiftly up his arm, across his shoulders and down the arm to the hand on her head.

She felt a sudden jolt. It snapped her head back, paralysing her, turning her body rigid. Her skin tingled. A shot of pain surged through her teeth as if she had just bitten up to her gums into a scoop of ice cream. She tried to cry out but her jaw was locked. Not only her jaw, but every bone in her body felt as if it had been turned to stone. The pain was excruciating. Her skin burned. It felt as if her flesh was being peeled from her body.

She tried clasping her eyelids together. She could not. Against her will, her eyes were drawn to his. They were piercing, driving right through her. They had their own force. They tugged at her eyeballs, threatening to rip them from their sockets. Little sparks flew from his lashes. Cobalt arcs of electricity flashed around his sockets. They fanned out and swept across his head as though it was a plasma globe.

His words boomed in her head. 'Tell me, Anaïs. Where is your sister?'

The ground beneath her feet rocked. It rose, then suddenly fell. Initially Anaïs thought it was part of his force field. Then she realised otherwise. The tremor did not come from him. It came from an outside source. The surge of earth beneath them lifted both of them into the air, the ground disappearing under their feet.

He continued to hold her gaze, yet his eyes were no longer piercing. Momentarily filled with surprise, they were soon charged with fear. While still airborne, he released her head, and with it the powerful physical hold he had over her.

The electrical charge coursing through her body ceased, but not the lack of control. Instead of rigid, she was now limp. Numb. Helpless. She fell backwards. The last thing she saw before hitting the ground and blacking out was another figure perched high above her.

Balanced precariously, with one foot on the eroded pinnacle of a stone archway, stood a woman wearing a black fedora. Her mouth and nose were obscured by a thick, black scarf. The rest of her face was as pale as porcelain.

RESCUE

The blackout was momentary. Anaïs snapped her eyes open. From her prone position, lying flat on her back, she watched the battle ensue.

Over the Ethnarch's shoulder Anaïs could see her—the mysterious woman in the fedora. How she managed to stay on what little remained of the rounded archway was miraculous. Save for the particularly large keystone positioned at the apex, there was barely anything substantial left of the structure. The keystone rocked and pivoted on the supporting stones. Atop it, the woman stood solid and secure, her torso almost motionless, while underneath her the entire archway swayed from side to side. However, her stance was not the most mind-boggling act she performed.

Rays of white heat shot from her fingertips. Each ray, brighter than the previous one and increasing steadily, flew directly at the Ethnarch. He used his tattered promptuary as a shield. Each time a bolt hit it, the star on its cover flashed. Sparks flew from its points.

A shower of them cascaded over his shoulders, dousing Anaïs in fiery particles. They pricked at her exposed skin like the points of needles. She drew up her knees, curled into a ball, and pulled her collar up over her cheek to protect her face.

As Deus attempted to dodge the bolts of light he danced from side to side. Each time he moved he exposed the little witch. When in the direct line of sight of the woman, Anaïs felt her tremendous power. A wave of it swept over her. With it came a blast of pure white-hot heat. She felt what the other woman felt. Anaïs sensed her rage. The malice, bitterness and pain were palpable. The woman had clearly been hurt. Badly. She was out for revenge.

The woman's emotions overwhelmed Anaïs. They came as a deluge. Such agony. More than anything Anaïs herself had ever experienced. Heart wrenching. Such was the force of emotion, the air became thick with it. A dark cloud formed behind the woman, framing her and adding to the weight of the emotions.

The only feeling Anaïs could compare it to was the moment Nan had died. The memory flashed through her mind. It played out like a jittery, grainy old movie, skipping the occasional frame. She saw the frantic search in the rubble for the caretaker's body. Her feelings of hopelessness and desperation were real once more. Their awfulness painfully tangible. She saw the moment Nan's lifeless corpse had been revealed. The anguish increased. No pain had ever been so great and so overwhelming.

Tears welled in the witch's eyes, misting her view.

Everything blurred. She slapped her palms against her sockets. She drew them back across her cheeks towards her ears. The salty water went with them. Drying instantly, the streaks pulled the skin taut across her face.

She was not alone with tears.

They streamed from the eyes of the woman balanced precariously on the arch. Eyes which Anaïs now saw clearly. The same eyes which had been mere centimetres from her own moments before the apartment in Amsterdam had collapsed. Moments before Nan's death. The death she had caused. The transfer of emotions swapped. Now the rage was Anaïs's.

The other woman felt it directed towards her. It distracted her. She took her eyes off the Ethnarch and stared at Anaïs. For an instant their eyes locked onto one another. She spluttered on her tears and averted her gaze. Anaïs watched her knot her brow, concentrate, and fire one last salvo at the Ethnarch.

The ray hit the ground at his feet. Splintering the rocky ground, it sent tiny shards of stone flying in all directions. A shower of them peppered Anaïs. The force of the impact launched him high into the air. It sent him sailing over the escarpment wall beside the little witch. To her amusement he let out what could best be described as a Wilhelm Scream.

The woman glanced back at Anaïs. She sighed and looked forlornly at the little witch, letting her arms fall limply by her sides. Anaïs felt the woman let go of her energy. It ebbed. It was a mistake. Distracted, with her focus on Anaïs, the force keeping her upright faltered.

With nothing supporting it the arch beneath her gave way. Anaïs watched as first the lower stones collapsed, quickly followed by the keystone. The woman went down with it. A huge cloud of dust rose to replace it. The cloud obscured everything. It burgeoned. Sweeping outwards, it rolled over the little witch.

Blinded by dust, Anaïs choked on it. She drew her scarf up over her nose and mouth. She turned her face to the side, screwed her eyes shut and held her breath. Drawing her coat up over her head, she shielded it. Another shower of stones rained down on her. And then another.

Anaïs waited for the destruction to subside. Before long it did.

Feeling no more stones hitting her and satisfied it was safe, she peeked out from under her coat. The cloud had settled. She wet her lips and wiped her mouth with the back of her hand. Tasting only dust, she spat out a glob of it. She coughed to clear her throat.

Propping herself up on her elbows, she took in her surroundings. Only remnants remained of what had been a relatively well-preserved ancient ruin. A thick layer of powdery, pale-yellow dust coated everything. Apart from the rubble, Anaïs was alone.

RUINS

The little witch attempted to extract herself from the rubble. Half buried, her lower legs were pinned under pulverised rock. She squirmed and writhed in an attempt to free herself. The weight of the rock was significant. Eventually she managed to dislodge enough rubble to turn herself over and wiggle out from under it.

She stood. A noise behind her drew her attention. Half expecting to see Deus Dominus and mentally preparing herself for battle as she did, she twirled around. To her relief, it was not him.

Ella and the shades emerged from the tunnel.

The Apothecary massaged her eyes, then blinked several times. Adjusting her eyesight to the outdoor glare, she surveyed her surroundings and whistled loudly. 'Wow! What happened here?'

'You don't want to know,' murmured Anaïs.

Ella ran her eyes over the little witch's clothing. Not

only her attire, but also her face and hair, were coated in an even layer of fine powder. 'You look like a ghost.'

'Very funny,' said the witch sarcastically. She pinched the breast pockets of her coat and shook it in an unsuccessful attempted to dust herself off.

The shades joined the Apothecary in appraising the witch.

'Are you okay, Anaïs?'

Anaïs sent her thoughts out to her caretaker. *'I think so, Nan.'*

'You should see yourself. You look like a ghost.'

'Ella just said that!' Anaïs retorted with irritation, before realising the caretaker was joking. She grinned in return and jibed her. *'You should speak for yourself.'*

She jumped on the spot, shaking more dust off her coat. She opened her coat and rubbed her hands on her pants to clean them. She then wiped her face. The wet dirt created by her sweaty palms left black streaks across her cheeks.

'I don't think that's going to work,' said Ella, scrutinising the witch. 'You're just spreading it around. Probably easier to hose you down.'

Licking her lips, Anaïs tasted the dust. 'Mmm, maybe you're right.' The gritty substance ground on her teeth as she rubbed them together. She snorted and spat out a glob of it. It raised a puff of powder as it hit the ground at her feet.

'Anaïs!'

Sheepishly, she glanced sideways at her caretaker. *'Sorry, Nan.'* She turned her attention back to the

Apothecary. 'We need to get out of here before he comes back.'

'He?' Ella's eyes widened. 'Was it the guy with the dogs again?'

'No,' said Anaïs, grimly shaking her head. 'Much worse. His father.'

Ella's eyes darted around the ruins. 'Great! You mean there's more of them?'

'Unfortunately, yes,' said Anaïs. She surveyed the ruins. 'Any idea how we can get out of here?'

'Nope.' Ella shrugged. 'Like I said before, I've only ever stopped for pizza in Catania. I've never been anywhere else on the island. Where are we anyway?'

'The promptuary said before that we were in a place called Taormina,' said Anaïs.

'I think we need more than a place name.'

Anaïs retrieved the handbook from her coat pocket. 'Let me have a look.' She commanded the promptuary, 'Map.'

The handbook responded as before, creating a three-dimensional image of their surroundings.

'Look,' said Ella. 'There's a train station.'

'I see it, but it's down at the foot of the hill. I don't want to go there.' She moved to the stone wall and peered over it. 'That's where I saw him go. We're certain to run into him that way.'

'Then we go back to the boat.'

'No, that was a dead end, and besides, there's a bunch of corpses down there. I really don't want to face that again.'

Ella eyed the entrance to the tunnel. 'Okay, I agree. But what do you want to do then? Fly?'

'That would be cool. Do you have something which can do that?'

The Apothecary shook her head. 'I wish. You saw my attempt with the broomstick on Malta. But even if it did work—which it doesn't—it's not here, is it?'

Anaïs sighed heavily. 'We can't hang around too long. Guys with dogs or not, we're going to have other problems soon. We'll have to deal with naturals as well. I'm sure destroying part of a monument will not go unnoticed.'

'Monument?'

'Yes, a minute ago this was the entrance to what looked like some kind of ancient amphitheatre.'

Ella stared at the mound of rubble, trying to visualise what it once may have looked like. 'You destroyed an amphitheatre?'

'No! Of course not!' Anaïs frowned. 'It was someone else. No time to explain. At any rate, if we hang around here too long, we'll get the blame for it.' Her frustration got the better of her. 'C'mon! Someone think of something!'

'What about this?'

Anaïs turned to face Joan. She had completely forgotten about the other shade. The body builder stood a few metres away next to a crevice. Anaïs scampered over a small mound of rubble and stood next to the shade. Both peered into the hole. A section of pathway had collapsed, revealing a stone stairwell.

The witch's eyes lit up. She grinned broadly. 'Cool!'

She moved to give Joan a hug of joy before thinking better of it. *Too cold.* She cleared her throat. 'Thanks, Joan.'

Nan and Ella joined Anaïs and Joan. The four of them stood in a circle around the hole.

'Right!' exclaimed Anaïs, clapping her hands together and raising a dust cloud from her coat. 'Let's go!'

'Go?' The Apothecary gave the crevice a dubious glance. 'You don't know where it leads.'

Anaïs rolled her eyes. 'Welcome to my world. I never know where I'm going. Just go with the flow. It looks like it goes down the hill and we will be out of sight. What more could we want?'

'But there might be more of them there.' She cocked her head at the tunnel full of corpses behind her.

'No choice. We'll tackle that when we come to it. We just have to keep moving.' Anaïs did not wait for a response. She slammed the handbook shut, dropped it into her pocket and sat down. She slid towards the hole and cast her legs over the edge. She leaned forward and pushed herself off, dropping down onto the top step.

She looked up at the faces staring down at her. Framed by the entrance to the crevice and towering behind them was the peak of Mount Etna. Disturbingly, it appeared to be spewing more smoke.

Anaïs beckoned frantically to the others. 'Well? What are you waiting for? Let's go.'

DESCENT

The deeper Anaïs went, the darker it became. The steps of the circular staircase were damp and slippery, making progress slow. She gripped the central stone pylon for support. As she descended it grew colder. The familiar musty smell of the previous tunnel returned.

Reaching the base of the staircase she stepped off the bottom tread into pitch black. Feeling around with her feet she sensed a smooth floor. She moved forward, waving her arms, but encountered no obstacles. She stopped to listen to the footfalls of the others as they reached the lower steps.

'Where are we now? The centre of the earth?' joked Ella from above.

'I don't think so. It would be a damn sight warmer,' replied Anaïs. 'Joan? I need light. Can you help?'

Anaïs heard a grunt and then the shade illuminated herself centimetres from Anaïs's face. Not feeling the usual cold aura from the shade because of the ambient temperature, nor expecting the shade to be so close, the witch drew in a sharp breath. In shock she jumped backwards and collided with a wall. She jarred her head on a low-hanging stone beam jutting out from it.

'Ow!'

'What's wrong Anaïs?'

'Oh, nothing, Joan.' She massaged her head, taking a moment to compose herself. 'You took me by surprise.'

'Excuse moi.'

'No problem. Thanks for the light. Let's keep going.' She looked over the shade's glowing shoulder. Nan stepped down into the tunnel, trailed by the Apothecary. There was a concerned look on Ella's face. 'Are you okay, Ella?'

'Yes,' ventured the Apothecary hesitantly. She surveyed the tight confines of the tunnel. In the glow of the shade the state of the tunnel was apparent. Constructed entirely of large blocks, the ceiling was missing substantial chunks of stonework. In the gaps loose earth trickled to the floor. It looked as if the ceiling would collapse at any moment.

'Is it safe?' enquired Ella.

'Dunno,' said Anaïs. She eyed a stone block at her feet which she had somehow managed to avoid tripping over. 'But I don't want to find out. It's probably not a good idea to hang around in here too long.'

'I'm with you.' Not having Anaïs's diminutive stature, Ella had to bend forward to fit in the tunnel. With hands on her knees she glanced at the same block. 'We better get moving. Besides, this is killing my back.'

Anaïs nodded. She ushered Joan in front of her. *'Can you lead the way?'*

'Ahem—'

'It will be fine, Joan. I'll be right behind you.'

'I don't know how long I can keep this up.' The shade sounded out of breath.

'Just do your best, Joan. We'll deal with that problem when we get to it.'

Joan nodded. The light from the movement of her head flashed across the brickwork, casting eerie shadows. Without a word she took her first tentative steps down the tunnel. Gradually she gained confidence and moved faster, picking up the pace. Anaïs followed. She struggled to keep up. Underfoot the surface became uneven, and she had to pay close attention to where she placed her feet. This slowed her down. The deeper they went into the tunnel, the greater the gaps in the ceiling. Stone blocks littered the floor of the already confined space. How the whole thing stayed up mystified Anaïs. With no time to dwell on it, she kept going. Her progress was slowed even more by having to pick her way between the blocks.

She heard Joan's breathing change. First, she began to pant. Eventually she was gasping from exertion.

'Joan, if you need a break we can stop.'

'No,' hissed the shade breathlessly. *'Just a little further. I think I see a door.'*

'A door?'

'Oui. Look. There.'

Joan stepped to one side and Anaïs saw it. A few steps in front of them the tunnel ended. Set in the wall, and perfectly formed in the arched shape of the tunnel, was a wooden door. In the centre was a large brass door knob.

Anaïs heard the shade expel her breath. Instantly, they were plunged into darkness. *'Sorry,'* was all she managed to pant.

'Nothing to be sorry about, Joan. You got us there. Or at least, you got us somewhere.' Anaïs listened for footsteps. She heard the scrape of shoes on loose stone. Then silence as they stopped. 'Nan? Ella? Are you still with us?'

'Yes,' they chimed together.

The sound of the Apothecary's and Nan's voices mixing in her head was disconcerting. Anaïs tapped her skull and cleared her throat. 'Good,' she said. 'I think we've found a way out.'

So close it was practically in Anaïs's ear, Ella sighed loudly with relief.

Anaïs gasped. 'Whoa!'

'What's wrong?'

'I thought you were back down the tunnel.'

'Sorry to disappoint you,' chirped Ella. 'We're both right here,'

'I can't see a thing. It's all very confusing.'

'You're not kidding,' said Ella. 'And now?'

'Hang on.' Using the shade's frozen aura as a guide, Anaïs shuffled past Joan. She moved towards the door, feeling her way by tapping a foot in front of her. Reaching out she felt the rough surface of the door. She slid her hand across it, searching for the door knob. She yelped.

'Anaïs?' cried Nan. *'What is it? Are you okay?'*

'Yes, Nan. No reason to panic. Just a splinter.' She gnawed on the soft tissue of her middle finger to soothe it against the offending object. She patted the door cautiously with her other hand until she found the knob. It turned easily. She pushed, but it would not budge. 'I need a little help here.'

Ella squirmed past Joan, joining Anaïs at the door. Nestled beside her, she could feel the Apothecary's hot breath on her cheek.

'Cosy,' joked Anaïs.

Ella chuckled and slung an arm around her shoulder. 'Very.'

'Right! Together! Push!'

With their combined weight the door yielded easily, swinging open. Both of them tumbled forward onto a tiled floor. Huddled together, with their legs tangled, they felt a number of hard objects rain down on them.

Oh, no! A cave-in!

Curiously the objects did not have the heaviness of stone. They were relatively light, and some made a metallic clang as they bounced off them onto the floor. A series of loud crashes followed. Ella and Anaïs clung tightly to one another, sheltering their heads with their arms. More objects fell on them. These were even lighter, surprisingly soft, and barely made a sound on impact.

Whatever was collapsing eventually ceased.

Anaïs extracted herself from Ella. She struggled to her feet and stood in a sea of metal and plastic containers. There seemed to be buckets everywhere. *Where are we? In a swimming pool?* The room was dimly lit and tiny. She estimated it to be only about a couple of metres square.

She glanced back at the shades. They stood in the door opening. Reading their eyes, she saw that they both seemed as perplexed as she was. She faced the opposite direction. Before her was another, more modern door. She waded the few steps towards it through the knee-high junk.

She cracked the door open. Outside a cacophony of noise and congestion took Anaïs by surprise. She slammed it shut. Turning, she rested her back against it.

'What is it?' exclaimed Ella, still half buried under containers.

'I think we will need a moment,' said Anaïs. 'We're not alone.'

THE STOREROOM

The little witch cracked the door open once more. She peered outside. Anaïs scratched her head, slightly nonplussed.

'Where are we?' enquired Ella.

Anaïs closed the door and turned to face her, her eyes darting around the room. 'I think right now we're in a cleaner's storage closet.'

Now standing, Ella joined Anaïs in appraising the room. She stood knee-deep in a mass of buckets, bottles, mops and, most of all, an incredible amount of toilet paper. Shelving which had been in front and beside the door to the tunnel had collapsed, causing the shambles. 'I can see that,' she said. 'But where are we exactly?'

'I'll check,' said Anaïs. She searched her coat pockets and pulled out her promptuary. She opened it and commanded the book to display a map of their location. The promptuary did as before, generating a holographic image of their surroundings. The image slowly turned, allowing her to view it in detail.

'Okay,' said Anaïs, twisting her lips. 'We're at a railway station. Zoom out and show me Immi.' The promptuary did as requested, displaying the station, nearby coastline and the city of Catania. A flashing purple dot appeared in the centre of the city. 'Looks pretty simple. If we catch a train here'—she pointed at their location and traced her finger along the railroad tracks—'it will take us back to Immi. Or at least get us close.'

'Let's do it then,' said Ella brightly.

Anaïs scrutinised the image. The promptuary displayed their surroundings in real-time. There were a lot of people milling around on the platform. 'It's pretty busy.'

'All the better,' said Ella. 'We can slip out of here and blend in.'

'Yes, we can do that. But what about them?' Anaïs indicated Nan and Joan. Both shades hovered in the doorway.

'They look fine to me.'

'Squeezing into a full train might give us problems. Have you ever gotten close to them. They're freezing.'

'I don't see the problem,' said Ella. 'It's winter.'

Anaïs shrugged. 'Fine. I guess you're right.'

'Then we just need tickets.'

'Tickets?'

'Train tickets,' said Ella. 'We don't want to complicate matters further by having to deal with a conductor.'

'Oh, yes, you're right.'

'I'll get them,' said Ella.

'Maybe it's not necessary,' said Anaïs. 'I've never tried it before. Let's see if the promptuary can do it.' She pointed at the circling image. 'Perhaps it can make something for real. It seems to be expanding its talents.'

'Okay, give it a go,' said Ella.

Gripping the handbook tightly, Anaïs closed her eyes. She cleared her head and concentrated. She pictured herself walking across the platform. Upon finding it, Anaïs stepped up to the ticket booth. She ordered tickets for her, Ella and the shades. To her amusement, the words coming out of her mouth were in Italian. The agent handed her the tickets.

She opened her eyes. The image floating before her above the handbook dematerialised. As if blown by an invisible wind, its pages began to flutter. They proceeded to flip rapidly. Zipping through the entire book, they whirred and clacked like the wonky blades of an old ventilator striking its safety cover as they twirled around.

The promptuary snapped shut in her hand. Holding it by the spine Anaïs extended her free hand and held it above the book. The promptuary emitted a loud 'cha-ching!' Four tickets shot up from between the pages

'Ha!' exclaimed Ella. 'Now that's magic!'

'Indeed!' Anaïs grinned. 'Excellent!' She pulled out the tickets. Nan and Joan entered the room, struggling to make their way through the shambles on the floor. Anaïs distributed the tickets.

'I don't think we should leave it like this,' said Ella, taking in the mess around her.

'You're right.' Anaïs eyed her handbook. 'While we're experimenting, let's see what else you can do.' She opened the promptuary and commanded it, 'Tidy!'

Instantly, everything on the floor lifted into the air. The door to the tunnel slammed shut. The shelves which had concealed the secret door levitated and slotted themselves back into position on their supports, disguising the entrance once more. Bottles which had spilled refilled themselves and replaced their caps. Toilet paper which had unrolled, rerolled itself onto its tubes. Plastic packaging which had split and strewn its contents across the floor reassembled itself and resealed. All the objects which had been on the shelving flew back onto the planks. The buckets, mops, and brooms slid across the room and set themselves in their rightful positions. They slid around, organising themselves into neat rows. The last object, an ancient vacuum cleaner, trundled into a corner on its squeaky wheels. The room fell silent.

Anaïs beamed. 'Nice!'

'Wow!' Ella returned the expression. 'Can I have one of those? She pointed at the handbook. 'Trying to keep my workshop clean and orderly is a royal pain.'

'Sorry, can't help you there,' said Anaïs with a smirk. 'Unfortunately, you don't qualify for one. It's a witch thing.'

'Pity.'

'I'll tell you what,' said Anaïs cheerfully. 'Next time you want to do a spring clean, let me know and I'll drop by.'

'Thanks.'

'No worries. It's the least I can do considering what you've done for me.'

'Good to know,' said Ella.

Anaïs swept the room with her eyes. 'Right! Enough of this. We're done here. Let's catch a train.'

THE POWER OF A BOOK

Previously, I touched on the existence of a promptuary which had fallen into the hands of naturals. The Voynich Manuscript has perplexed researchers for centuries. It is rumoured to be the property of one Cornelis Drebbel. Whether this is indeed a fact, nobody in the present witch community knows for certain.

Assuming this information was a closely guarded secret, then unfortunately the knowledge of its true owner has been taken to the grave. But it would go a long way to explaining the special properties of this manuscript. It would also explain why it has been stripped of its cover and tampered with. Presumably in order to prevent it from functioning.

All things aside, the manuscript itself is far less intriguing than its owner. As with all promptuaries, they can only function properly in the hands of their rightful owner.

Cornelis Drebbel was a Dutch inventor—and a

witch. This much is fact. He has infamously gone down in the annals of witch history as one of the few witches who harnessed the full capabilities of their promptuary. His talents were such that, in his care, his handbook became a super promptuary.

With its help he created all manner of weird and wonderful objects. Among his inventions were a magic lantern, a camera obscura, microscopes and a solar-powered harpsichord. Further unleashing the talents of his promptuary, he invented an incubator, thermostats, and an air-conditioner powered by salt. He also created a *perpetuum mobile*—a perpetual motion machine—and, in so doing, defied the natural laws of thermodynamics.

Cornelis dabbled in explosives. He produced torpedoes, naval mines and fulminating gold. This last form of explosive produced purple fumes, something which would have pleased Anaïs no end. He even constructed several navigating submarines.

Naturally the witch community was more than pleased with the ingenuity of his inventions. Except, of course, for the solar-powered harpsichord, for which they had very little use. Witches love music as much as the rest of us, but none of them have the time to learn an instrument.

The community marvelled at how incredibly in sync he was with his promptuary. Even to the point of creating jealousy in the ranks. Setting jealousy aside, there was one much more serious problem. Cornelis's penchant for invention got the better of him.

He flaunted his talents before the general public. In particular before royalty across Europe. His fame spread far and wide. He broke the fundamental rules of witch secrecy. He went as far as to astound naturals by producing thunder and lightning on command. This raised the ire of witchdom. Although his talents were vast, the good of the whole community took precedence. Eventually they were forced to step in and put a stop to his antics.

Rumour has it that the extreme step of separating him from his promptuary was taken. Something which is virtually impossible. Promptuaries never want to leave their owners. In the case of Cornelis, the witch community found a way. Naturally those who hit upon the solution would not want this to be common knowledge. The details have never been disclosed to the wider community.

A promptuary and its owner are intrinsically linked. Separation from it, or Disunion, as it is called, is no easy feat. It is not surprising that the means to achieving this have never been revealed. This knowledge could bring about the end of witchdom if it fell into the wrong hands. For Cornelis it meant ostracisation from the community. Without a promptuary his witch powers virtually disintegrated. He was relegated to living out his days in obscurity. The lifespan of a witch is long. Without the ability to practise his craft, his final years must have been a trauma to endure.

As Anaïs grows and develops, so does her promptuary. It is clearly apparent, after her adventures in the tunnels of Sicily, that she is steadily becoming one with her handbook. However, like Cornelis Drebbel, she must to be careful not to fall into using it for party tricks and such. Nor should the existence of such a truly powerful form of magic be revealed to naturals.

With great power comes responsibility. Being a witch does not absolve you from punishment. The rest of the witch community will see to that. When power is abused it will invariably be removed.

RUSH HOUR

Anaïs waited with the others in the storage room until the train arrived. As soon as its doors opened they scooted across the platform and crammed themselves in with the other passengers. The train was packed, filled with a mixture of tourists and commuters. There was very little seating, leaving Anaïs and the shades standing room only. As Anaïs had predicted, the shade's chill proved to be a problem. Their frozen auras caused people to retract from them.

She chuckled as she watched their reactions. *Naturals! Ha! If only they knew.* Fortunately, it had a positive side-effect. It gave them more room to move through the crowded carriage. Finding a spot towards the rear, they huddled in a group next to a man who appeared to be impervious to the cold. He did not move when they crowded him for space. Assuming he was a shade, and taking no chances, Anaïs avoided engaging him. Thankfully he ignored her, lost in his own private oblivion. She had more than enough to deal with as it was.

The journey seemed to take forever. Anaïs squeezed between the others and found a section of wall to lean against. She toasted herself above a heater positioned at her feet. It was warm—a little too warm. The rocking to and fro, combined with the heat, began to lull her to sleep. That was until the train lurched to one side. She toppled over, falling into Nan's arms. The shade's icy touch snapped her awake.

'Oops,' muttered Anaïs. She rubbed her eyes. 'Sorry, Nan.'

'It's okay, Anaïs. If you want to sleep, you can.'

Anaïs sent her thoughts back. *'Mm … no. I'd better not. Do you remember the trip from England?'* Nan batted her eyes in affirmation. *'I slept for a week. Probably not such a good idea to do that right now. Especially considering what happened then. What if I started transforming in front of them?'* She cast a furtive eye around the carriage.

'No, I agree. You're right. Probably not a good idea.' Nan sniggered. *'Besides, when you sleep; you sleep like the dead. Waking you is impossible.'*

Anaïs smiled. *'Funny you of all people would come out with that expression.'*

'Never thought about it that way.' Nan snorted softly. *'Maybe I'm getting used to this.'*

Anaïs rummaged in her beret and pulled out her sunglasses. She slipped them on and appraised the real Nan. Jokingly, she nudged the caretaker with her elbow. *'I have to admit, you look pretty good considering your condition.'*

Nan grinned. *'Good to know. I'm feeling a lot better now.'*

'Definitely not like when you were with the hellhounds?'

'No, definitely not.' A pained expression clouded the caretaker's face. *'That was terrible.'*

'Yes, you looked terrible. I thought I was going to lose you.' Anaïs paused, reflecting on their experiences with the Inquisitor. The image of Nan lying helpless on the stone slab masquerading as a makeshift altar in the volcano's crater, flashed through her mind. She gulped. That had been too close. *'What was it like?'*

Nan raised an eyebrow. *'What was what like?'*

'You know, being in the grip of one of those things—a hellhound. How did it feel?'

'I'm not sure how to describe it. I suppose it's a lot like the way a battery feels. Slowly being drained.' She twisted her lips. *'Basically, I was paralysed and had no control over anything. Kind of just floating there. And it hurt like hell.'* She tapped her sternum. *'There was a burning sensation in my chest. Like a fire sucking up all the oxygen. But worse than that, it felt as if as I was being ripped apart. Like it was trying to turn me inside out. It took all my willpower to keep the force, or whatever it was, at bay.'*

Anaïs chewed her bottom lip. She sighed deeply. The breath caught in her throat. She choked. Tears welled in her eyes. *'I'm sorry, Nan. Sorry that I ever let that happen to you.'*

'Oh, Anaïs, it's not your fault.' She slung an arm around the witch.

The tears on the little witch's face crystallised into ice. For once, Anaïs did not feel the cold. Her thoughts were elsewhere,

'You can't take responsibility for their actions,' continued Nan. *'You are not in the wrong here. None of this is your fault.'*

'But—'

'We're caught up in something much bigger than you or I. That's clear now. But if we stick together ... ' Her eyes darted from the little witch to Joan and then to Ella. *' ... all of us, then we can get to the bottom of this. But first we need to get as far away from them as possible.'*

'First we have to find Immi.'

'Well, that shouldn't be too hard.' Nan smiled. *'It's not like she's capable of keeping a low profile.'*

Anaïs smirked. *'At the moment she doesn't have a choice.'*

'Oh?'

Anaïs nodded. *'We locked her away for safekeeping.'*

'Really? How did you manage that?'

'Long story,' Anaïs smiled and cleared her throat. *'But we can kill two birds with one stone. Where she is, is also our way out of here.'*

Anaïs's attention was drawn to a commotion further down the train. A group of passengers staring out a window on the opposite side of the carriage gasped simultaneously.

The Apothecary moved between the witch and Nan, blocking Anaïs's view. Irritated, Anaïs opened her mouth to complain.

Ella bent to peer out the window. Her expression changed abruptly, her jaw dropped, her face turning white. 'Oh no!'

Anaïs manoeuvred her way around Ella. She followed the Apothecary's gaze. Narrowing her eyes, she peered through the window at Mount Etna's summit. Anaïs's complexion paled, matching that of the Ella's. A colossal plume of black smoke spewed from the mountain. It filtered what little sunlight there was, casting a dark shadow over everything.

ERUPTION

A tremendous thump sent shockwaves through the soles of Anaïs's boots. Shortly afterwards came the sound of a distant explosion. Anaïs felt the floor beneath her lift. The hypnotic hum of the train's wheels rolling on the rails ceased, the sound stuttering and then stopping completely. A strange silence prevailed.

Time slowed for Anaïs. The carriage seemed airborne for an eternity. Yet it all occurred in a split second. The train crashed back down, throwing many of the passengers off their feet. Miraculously it realigned itself on the rails, the flanges on its wheels screaming in protest.

Careening from side to side, Anaïs felt the vehicle lose momentum. In the driver's cabin, the impact of the train landing bounced the operator out of his chair, causing him to release the dead man's switch. The ear-splitting screech of brakes pierced Anaïs's ears.

In the carriage the passengers were thrown violently

forward. The screams of horror were so loud they even drowned out the sound of the brakes. Those seated smashed into the backs of the seats in front of them. The rapid deceleration sent those still standing tumbling to the floor and sliding to the front of the carriage, Anaïs and her companions included. At the head of the carriage the force compacted their bodies into a tight bunch against the wall.

Within moments the train came to a complete standstill. Cocooned by the bodies of her companions, Anaïs escaped her forward tumble unscathed. A passing thought caused her to giggle nervously at the absurdity of the situation. *Wow! Who would have guessed shades would make such good cushions.* Jammed between Nan and Joan, she attempted to still her chattering teeth. Wiggling free, she extracted herself from the jumble of limbs. Clambering to her feet, she helped Ella do the same.

With her heart pounding, and panting from the exertion, she glanced out the window. The black cloud above the volcano had expanded exponentially, now practically blocking out all sunlight. Out of it, in the surreal twilight, rocks and other debris were jettisoned into the air. The little witch watched dumbfounded as a mass of it flew towards them.

Within moments the debris rained down on the carriage. Fine pellets peppered the metal roof above her, sounding for all the world like a hailstorm. Only one vastly more intense than she had ever experienced. Anaïs ducked instinctively and covered her head.

The Apothecary was beside herself. Her eyes wild,

she cried out in panic. 'Anaïs! How do we get out of here? Where do we go?'

Masking her own apprehension, and taken aback by the Apothecary's unsurprising yet uncharacteristic reaction, Anaïs tried to calm her. 'Chill, Ella. Hang on. Give me a moment.'

She fumbled in her pocket. Her own nerves got the better of her. Frantically, she tried to extract the promptuary but could not free it. In her haste it caught in the folds of the pocket's loose inner lining.

'Anaïs, stop.' Nan, now standing beside her, whispered softly, *'Take your time. Take a deep breath. Try to relax.'*

Nan's calming voice did its job. Suppressing her anxiety, Anaïs closed her eyes and blocked out the chaos around her. She stopped tugging on the book. Composing herself, she slowly pulled it out of her pocket, slightly surprised at how easily it cooperated. She opened her eyes and stared down at the book in her hands before turning to the caretaker. *'Thanks, Nan.'*

Nan winked at her. *'Don't mention it. Always willing to be of service.'*

Anaïs slid the sunglasses up the bridge of her nose. She smiled at the shade. 'If you put it that way, then I'm always willing to oblige,' she joked.

'Sorry?' said Ella. 'Did you say something?'

'Oh, no, it's nothing.' She went to open the promptuary. 'Let's see where we are and find the best way out of here.'

'Um … hold on,' said Ella, grabbing her arm to stop her opening the book. 'Don't you think the other passengers will think it a bit weird? You know, your you-know-what doing its you-know-thing?'

'Ella, I don't think that's important right now,' murmured Anaïs through the corner of her mouth. 'I'm pretty sure they're otherwise occupied,'

A mountain of a man pried open the door nearest to them. The passengers began to exit the train. They were agitated and in a high state of alarm, and it did not go smoothly. Concerned only with their personal well-being, an altercation ensued between two women. Both crowned with towering beehives, with their hairdos in total disarray, they tried to force their way through the opening together. Not only their hairstyles, but also their attitude reminded Anaïs of the librarian. She shook her head in dismay. *Naturals!*

A fresh shower of stones rained down on the train. Outside, the passengers scattered in all directions, sheltering their heads with whatever protection they had—their coats, briefcases and umbrellas.

'Right!' said Anaïs. 'We've got to get out of here. Now!' She flipped open the promptuary and concentrated. 'Show me Immi.'

The handbook produced its three-dimensional image. Anaïs saw the train. Amazingly the carriages sat orderly lined up on the rails. Behind them the tracks were skewed and split apart, separated by a mound of earth which had risen between them. It was a miracle they had survived unharmed. In front of the train lay the city of Catania. It seemed unscathed for the moment. Most of the fallout from the volcano was landing on the outskirts. The flashing blip, which had to be Immi, was close. By her estimate, Anaïs guessed it would not take long to get to her location. However, getting there would depend on the fluctuating and unpredictable state of the erupting volcano. One thing was clear, they had to find a safe passage. It was up to her to guide them. She had to take charge.

Anaïs eyed Ella and the shades. 'Okay, I know where to go. Are we ready?'

'We better be,' said the Apothecary. She gave Anaïs a wink and managed to crack a thin smile. To Anaïs's relief Ella's optimistic attitude seemed to have returned. Dealing with a panic-stricken natural would have only made it all the more difficult.

Ella waited as the last passengers, a man and his daughter, climbed down from the wagon. She stuck her head out the door and glanced at the sky. It was as black as ink. The intermittent shower of stones had stopped. She glanced at Anaïs. 'Now's our chance.' The little witch nodded and Ella jumped from the wagon.

Anaïs moved to follow her. Stopping at the lip of the door, she stared down at the drop. 'Think I need a little help here,' she said, scratching her head.

'What's the problem?' said Ella jokingly. 'You're a witch. Fly!'

'Never a broomstick around when you need one,' replied Anaïs.

Ella flashed her a smile. 'All of a sudden you seem to have a thing for broomsticks. Why is that?'

'Dunno.' Anaïs shrugged. 'Maybe because of the one you have on Malta.'

'I'll work on it when I get back. C'mon then,' said Ella, opening her arms. 'I'll catch you.'

Anaïs hesitated, judging the distance to the Apothecary. Ella stood unsteadily on the sloped mound of rocks supporting the railway sleepers. She waved Anaïs towards her. Her position seemed a little too precarious. Anaïs glanced up at the ominous sky. *No choice in the matter.* She stuffed the promptuary into her pocket, took a deep breath and sprang down into the arms of the Apothecary.

'Oof!' exclaimed Ella as she caught the witch, sliding on the rocks and fighting to keep her balance. 'You're heavier than you look.'

'Must be the weight of my mental self,' muttered Anaïs.

'Sorry, did you say something?'

'Just thinking out loud,' said Anaïs.

'You better be careful doing that. You seem to talk to yourself a lot. Someone might think you're even stranger than you already are.'

'I don't think that's even a possibility,' said Anaïs. 'Thanks, Ella. You can put me down now.'

The Apothecary did as requested. Bending forward she set the little witch down on the rocks. The shades had also jumped from the train and joined them.

'So! Which way?' enquired Ella.

Anaïs pointed past the front of the train towards the city.

From above came the sound of whistling, not unlike that of a dive-bomber. A huge boulder, the size of a small car, landed behind them on the rear carriage of the train, crushing it flat. The sound of its impact was deafening. Splinters of rock and glass flew in all directions. Remarkably, none of it hit any of them, the carriage beside them offering some protection.

Instantly coated in sweat from the shock of what had happened, Anaïs felt her body for injuries. Discovering she was unharmed, she called out to Ella. 'Are you okay?'

The Apothecary had lost her footing on the rocky ballast supporting the train tracks. Her legs had gone out from under her and she had slid on her rear end to the bottom of the mound. She stood and massaged her bruised posterior.

'I'm fine,' said Ella, visibly shaken by the close call.

Anaïs eyed Ella for a moment. Satisfied the Apothecary was relatively unharmed, she cast the incident aside. *Forget it. Keep going.* She set her sights on the city and began marching towards it.

'Quick, let's get to shelter,' she said, waving to the others over her shoulder and nodding at the flattened carriage. 'Before something like that lands on us.'

DOWNTOWN

The streets of downtown Catania had looked relatively unscathed from the little detail the promptuary had shown her. Once Anaïs and her small party ventured among the buildings, it was evident this was not the case. It looked like a war zone.

The streets were deserted, the only indication of life, the sound of sirens in the distance. Debris from the volcano had wreaked massive destruction. A thick layer of stones and other rubble littered the streets. Entire buildings had collapsed. Others were threatening to do the same. Picking their way between the razed buildings and dodging what the sky fed them was a tough task.

The hard rain persisted. Stones of all shapes and sizes pelted down on them. Ella and Anaïs searched for shelter where they could find it. The shades walked unaffected through the torrent. Although seeming immune to the fallout, when the stones hit Joan, Anaïs heard the ringing of the rocks impacting her armour. *Strange*, she thought.

Cowering under the verandah of one of the few buildings still offering stable shelter—a solid stone structure with a line of massive columns—she discarded the thought and searched for her promptuary. She commanded it to display the librarian's location. She watched the dots of their and Immi's positions materialise.

'We're close,' she said to Ella. 'Just around the corner I think.'

'Good,' replied the Apothecary. 'The quicker we get out of this, the better.'

'You're not kidding.' Anaïs consulted the map. She cocked her head to the right. Sensing a lull, she took a step forward. 'This way,' she said.

Ella grabbed her by the elbow, holding her back. 'Wait.' She nodded at the sky. Hurled from the volcano and heading towards them was a fresh blizzard of rock. She ushered Anaïs behind a stone pillar. The moment they stepped behind it, an intense shower of stones hit, peppering it like bullets from a machine gun. The falling debris created a cloud of dust. It swept under the verandah, enveloping them completely. Huddled together, they covered their faces with their hands. The onslaught persisted.

'We can't stay here!' Ella yelled between her fingers. 'Let's get inside.'

Feeling her way with her free hand, she guided Anaïs across to a set of double glass doors. One of them was cracked open. At first it would not budge. Ella set her weight against it. Surprisingly it yielded easily.

They tumbled inside. Ella scrambled to her feet,

threw her body against the door and slammed it shut. Panting, she tried to catch her breath. She choked on the fine mist of dust hanging in the air. She convulsed. Sinking to her knees, she began to cough uncontrollably.

Anaïs drew her scarf up over her mouth and nose, tucking it under the rims of her sunglasses. She jammed her hand into her beret. Fumbling frantically she searched for a tiny item among all the other objects. Feeling its slender shape, she breathed a sigh and pulled out the drinking straw.

She offered it to the Apothecary. 'Here, Ella, breathe through this.'

Through the tears streaming down her face the Apothecary could not see a thing. Her convulsions were getting worse. Anaïs placed the straw in her hand and guided it to her mouth. She moved in close. Nestling her head next to Ella's, she whispered in her ear, 'Big breaths, Ella.'

The Apothecary did as instructed. She sucked on the straw. Firstly taking large gulps and then, as her panic subsided, she began to regulate her breathing. Ella dried her face, smearing it black with dust wet with tears.

'Better?' enquired Anaïs, her voice muffled by her makeshift mask.

The Apothecary nodded, sniffing loudly.

'Good,' said Anaïs. 'Hopefully if we go further inside the air will be more breathable.'

Before they could move there was a loud rapping at the door. Anaïs and Ella looked at each other in surprise. Anaïs walked across to the door and wiped dust from the glass with her sleeve. The shades stood on the other side. *Oops! Completely forgot about them.*

She opened the door. Nan and Joan slipped into the room, bringing with them a vast cloud of dust. It filled the space. Pinching her nose and holding the straw in the same hand, Ella slammed the door shut with her shoulder.

The cloud of dust settled somewhat. Anaïs glanced at the shades. *'Sorry, Nan.'*

'No need to apologise, Anaïs. Your safety is more important than ours.' She managed a weak smile. *'Even in this, not much harm can come to us.'*

'Right you are,' murmured Anaïs, relieved to be reunited with the shades, but cursing herself for forgetting them. 'Let's go inside.'

Turning, she led the way across the room and through another set of double doors. The others followed. Inside, they found a curved corridor decked out in plush red carpet. The dust followed them but was less than before.

Anaïs pushed on. The corridor was lined with doors on one side. *Are we in a hotel?* She tried several of them before finding one which opened. Together, they went through.

Anaïs's eyes widened. There were hundreds of chairs. Lined up in rows, they were covered in velvet the same red as the carpet. In fact, everything was red, except for the other predominant colour: gold. The air here was clearer. There was a fine mist of particles hanging in it, but nothing like where they had come from.

Ella took the straw out of her mouth. She coughed and cleared her throat. 'Wow!' she croaked, looking around them. 'I think we're in a theatre.'

'A pretty spectacular one at that,' said Anaïs, tilting her head back and admiring the rings of tiered balconies above her. The ceiling was covered in frescos and ornate pieces of sculptured plaster.

Ella handed the straw back to her. 'Thanks. You're a lifesaver.'

Anaïs grinned. 'Always willing to be of service. C'mon, let's try and find Immi.'

THEATRICS

Anaïs opened her handbook and commanded it to show their surroundings. The image the promptuary produced depicted the building in full three-dimensional detail. Anaïs could see the foyer they had come through; the auditorium and the corridor surrounding it; the stage and fly tower above it; and storage areas beneath the building. Deep in a cellar, the familiar flashing dot showing the librarian's location winked on and off.

'We got lucky,' said Anaïs. She nodded at the ceiling. 'We don't have to go out in that again.' She pursed her lips. 'A bit strange we can't hear it though.'

Ella shrugged. 'Soundproofing I suppose. We are in a theatre.'

'I guess you're right. Never thought about that.'

A muffled thud sounded. The auditorium lighting flickered. A large piece of sculptured cornice dislodged itself from the top of the proscenium. It crashed down on the front row of seating. Hitting the backs of the chairs it splintered in every direction. Anaïs and Ella ducked back under the balcony to avoid being hit by more pieces of falling plaster.

'I thought this place was solid,' murmured Anaïs.

'Obviously not solid enough,' said Ella. 'Good thing we weren't paying for those seats. I'd want my money back.'

'I think you'd have a hard time getting it,' quipped Anaïs in return.

'Once the two of you have stopped joking, can we get out of here?'

Anaïs turned to her caretaker. She read the concern in her eyes. *'Sorry, Nan, you're right.'*

'Ella,' said Anaïs, 'we better move.'

The Apothecary glanced above her. Cracks began forming in the ceiling. Small streams of white powder trickled from them like little waterfalls. 'Yes, and fast,' she said.

Anaïs scrutinised the promptuary's image. 'We have to go over the stage. By the looks of it we can get downstairs somewhere at the back.'

Ella swept her hand before her. 'Lead the way.'

'Easier said than done.'

'We don't have much choice, do we?'

Anaïs shook her head. Warily, she looked at the ceiling. The shower of plaster chunks had stopped. Holding the promptuary above her head for protection, Anaïs scooted down the centre aisle. Avoiding the damage in the front row, she shuffled along the second row across to a door at the side of the stage. She opened it and went through, followed by the others. Another piece of the proscenium broke off and fell onto the front of the stage with a loud crash.

Anaïs hesitated.

'Don't look, Anaïs. Keep going,' Ella urged her. 'We don't have long.'

Watching more plaster fall onto the seating, the little witch needed no further instruction. She climbed a small set of stairs leading to stage level and moved through the wings. She stopped for a moment. Taken by surprise at the sight of a statue of a giant angel in the dim light, Anaïs stood in shock, eyeing its proportions and lifelike appearance.

Another crash in the auditorium caused Ella to prod her in the ribs. 'No time for sightseeing.'

'Yes,' agreed Anaïs.

She shuffled past the angel and picked her way further upstage through the gloom. In contrast to the auditorium, the stage was unlit. Anaïs could barely see. There were lots of props and other paraphernalia. Many with sharp edges. It appeared as if the theatre had been abandoned in the middle of a performance.

'This place is more dangerous than outside,' said Anaïs

'I disagree,' said Ella as a resounding thud shook the building. They heard more plaster fall into the auditorium.

'Okay, you have a point.'

At the rear was a well-lit set of stairs. They led beneath the stage. Anaïs opened her promptuary and commanded it to display the location of Immi. The librarian was directly below them. She took the stairs, following them down under the stage. The smell of horse manure penetrated her nostrils. She pinched them.

'Man! What kind of shows do they put on here?'

Ella coughed. 'Beats me,' she said, her voice muffled by her hands which were cupped around her nose. 'Keep moving, will you.'

'Okay, okay!'

The promptuary guided Anaïs to a doorway on the other side of the cellar. Through it was another set of stairs.

Anaïs sighed loudly. 'Why can't someone think of putting an elevator in one of these places. If I have to climb any more stairs I'll go bonkers!'

'Stop complaining, Anaïs.'

The little witch pulled a face at her caretaker. Nan's eyes told her not to push the point. She picked her way down the stairs. The steps in the first level were wooden. Thereafter, they were hewn from stone.

At the bottom a rotten wooden door coated in a layer of moss barred her way. Anaïs gave it a half-hearted shove, expecting it to be non-responsive like the previous doors. Surprisingly it opened easily. Swinging slightly ajar, its lower hinges broke, leaving it hanging at an angle by its top hinge. She squeezed through the triangular gap onto a stone ledge.

To her amazement they were back in the underground waterway where they had found the Dreadnought. Only now the temperature was no longer cool, but very hot. Moisture dripped from the stone ceiling as if it too were perspiring. Anaïs wiped her brow.

The flow of water had not subsided. It rushed past her feet, licking the edge of the narrow walkway. She shimmied along it, careful not to lose her footing on the wet surface.

Using the dim light provided by the promptuary's image she searched for the entrance to where Immi was. She found the door with the star. She paused, taking a moment to reflect on where they had been since they were last here. And what they had been through: the battle with Deus and his son, the hellhounds, eruptions, the rising dead and the devastation raining down around them. It was a miracle they had survived. *Time to get off this island. I'm sure this is a great holiday destination, but it certainly hasn't lived up to it for me.*

'Well?' said Ella. 'Are we in the right place?'

'Huh?' The Apothecary's voice snapped her out of her thoughts. 'Oh sorry, yes.' She glanced at the map and pointed at the door. 'She should be here.' Repositioning herself on the walkway, Anaïs pounded the door with her fist. There was no response from the other side.

'Try it again,' said Ella.

Anaïs nodded. She tucked the handbook under her arm and hit the door again. This time harder, striking it with both fists. She stopped to listen. *Nothing.* Her trepidation grew. After a short moment of silence, she heard movement. Someone on the other side fumbled with the handle. A surge of panic swept over her. *Please, let it not be him.*

The door flew open. Anaïs let out a sigh of relief.

The librarian stepped into the doorway with her

hands on her hips, her face glowing red. Anaïs opened her mouth to greet her but was cut off.

'Where have you been?' yelled Immi. 'The whole place is coming down around our ears!'

'I'm well aware of that!' retorted Anaïs. She rolled her eyes. *I missed you too.* 'No time to explain. We're back now. Let's get the hell out of here!'

LEAVING CATANIA

Anaïs eyeballed the librarian. 'We can't get in if you stand in the way.'

Grudgingly, with a snarl on her face, Immi stepped aside to allow the others to enter.

Anaïs waited for them to pass and went to follow. An odd sound stopped her in her tracks. She looked down the tunnel. At first there was a distant rumble. Then a clattering, as if hard objects were being sucked up by through the tube of a vacuum cleaner. The clatter grew steadily in volume. Then it became a roar. Anaïs caught her breath.

Joan hung in the doorway. The little witch shoved her roughly aside as she pushed her way into the anteroom. She grabbed the door and slammed it shut, throwing her weight against it.

'Help!' she cried.

No one moved. The shades and Immi stood in confusion, the librarian mimicking the shade's comatose disposition.

'Hey!' yelled Anaïs frantically. 'Wake up you guys! Help me lock this!'

Ella sprang to her assistance, throwing her shoulder against the door. She searched for a way to secure it. Two ancient deadbolts were screwed to the wood. She slid them into their housings, catching her finger on one of them in the process.

'Ow!'

'What!' exclaimed Anaïs.

The Apothecary sucked on her finger. 'It's fine. Just my finger. No permanent damage.' She examined her digit.

From the other side came loud scraping and banging. The door began to vibrate. They both stepped away from it.

'Is someone out there?' enquired Ella.

Anaïs shook her head. 'Not someone … something.'

The noise grew. The roar Anaïs had heard before permeated the little room, filling it completely with sound. Combined with this came a loud swishing. The little witch glanced at the floor. Water seeped under the door and quickly rose to ankle depth. Anaïs looked up at Ella. 'Does that answer your question?'

Ella nodded vigorously. 'Let's get out of here.'

Ushering the others before them, Anaïs and Ella manoeuvred the shades and Immi out of the anteroom and into the main hall. They closed and secured the door to the anteroom. Rubber seals on the door prevented water from entering the room. The water which had flowed in gurgled down a drain in the centre of the main hall. Anaïs frowned. *Clearly this is not a first-time occurrence.*

The librarian was beside herself. 'Would someone please tell me what is going on?'

'I believe we are experiencing a natural disaster,' said Ella.

Immi cocked her head at the little witch. 'You mean her?'

Anaïs flushed red. 'What's your problem?'

'You,' said Immi flatly.

'What do mean, me?'

'I told you. I was stuck here for I-don't-know-how-long with what's-her-face.' Immi flicked a thumb at the child shade. 'It was as boring as hell. She's not exactly good company. You can't pass the time of day with someone who stares into space the whole time.'

'Right now I'd settle for that over you,' murmured Anaïs.

'What?' retorted Immi with fire in her eyes.

Although tempted to prolong the argument, Anaïs took a deep breath and fought the urge to respond. She gritted her teeth. *Don't do it.*

Ella came to her rescue. 'Guys! We don't have a lot of time.' She laid a hand on the witch's shoulder. 'Which way, Anaïs?'

The Apothecary's reassuring touch helped calm her. Anaïs considered their options. They could not return to Malta. The fallout from the volcano would surely affect that island as well. They would have to get further away. Anaïs eyed the symbols above the doors. Ella had previously said they were in Arabic but could not decipher them. None of them made any sense to Anaïs either.

Which one?

She pulled out the promptuary. *When all else fails, rely on magic.* Opening it she asked the book the same question. From the centre stitching between the pages an arrow formed. It rose above the handbook. Levitating, it began to spin around an invisible fulcrum.

'Great!' said Immi. 'Are we going to play roulette now?'

Anaïs cast her aside. *There's no arrow on a roulette wheel, you idiot.* She closed her eyes and concentrated, trying to envisage a place of safety. All she could come up with was the image of a tropical beach. One complete with palm trees, sparkling blue water and pristine white sand. She sighed. *Yeah, that would be nice. But—*

She opened her eyes. The arrow had stopped. It quivered, its point indicating a door on the far side of the room. Anaïs looked at the squiggle on its surface, but it gave no clues to what it meant. Printed in embossed lettering it read:

البندقية

'Looks like we have a destination,' said Anaïs. 'Do you know what it means, Ella?'

The Apothecary walked over to the door. She squinted at the symbol inscribed in it. 'Nope.' She indicated the symbol on the door which they had come through. 'I only know the symbol for exit and that is certainly not one.'

'I don't think it matters where it goes,' said Anaïs. 'We just need to get out of here.'

'Can't argue with that,' said Ella. 'Let's see if it works.'

The Apothecary opened the door and went into the anteroom. Anaïs followed. She recalled the tube from her previous visit, marvelling at the technology. *How does this all still work?* Running from wall to wall, an enormous brass tube filled most of the room. Above it a spaghetti of smaller tubes, resplendent with taps, dials and valves, filled the rest of the space. Most of them fed into the ceiling. A distant thud sounded. The earth beneath her trembled. The tubing rattled. Grit seeping between the tiles on the ceiling showered her from above.

Ella and Anaïs glanced at one another. They both dusted the grit from their hair. Wordlessly the Apothecary opened the tube. She pried open the large door embedded in its side. Pulling it towards her, she swung it around on its hinges and flat against the tube. The door made a resounding clang as it hit the outer wall. Ella twisted the star-shaped knob on the inner door and stood back to watch it slide upwards. She stepped inside the tube.

She turned to Anaïs. 'You get the others in here and I'll see if I can fire this thing up.'

The witch nodded.

Following Anaïs's instructions the shades seated themselves. Only Nan, who had not made the trip previously, questioned the sanity of what they were doing. *'Are you sure this is safe?'*

'We already survived a trip in one of these, Nan. I'm pretty sure we can survive another.' She glanced at the Apothecary

fiddling with dials on the console in front of her. *'That is, if Ella can get it working. I honestly don't know what else to do.'*

The floor beneath them rocked with another barrage from the volcano. The movement dislodged more refuse from the ceiling. A tile fell on the brass tube with an almighty clang. Nan needed no more encouragement. She quickly stepped into the tube and seated herself. Surprisingly, Immi uttered no complaint and silently followed the caretaker's lead.

What? Is she now going to be more cooperative? Anaïs watched Immi secure the shades in their seats before seating herself. Immi buckled herself in. Anaïs read fear in the librarian's face. *No, scared out of her wits. Not a permanent change.*

Anaïs closed the outer and inner doors. She sat behind Ella. Amplified by the confines of the small space, the noise in the tube caused by the reverberations from the volcano was tremendous. It sounded as if the whole world was caving in around them.

Over Ella's shoulder Anaïs watched as the Apothecary continued checking the dials on the console. They seemed to be functioning. She glanced upwards, visualising the devastation occurring on the surface. But for how long?

'Will it work?' enquired Anaïs.

'I hope so,' Ella said grimly. 'My Post-It notes are in the other tube, but I think I remember everything. If not, we're in for a world of pain.'

Anaïs eyed the curvature of the tube above her. 'If it's any consolation, I think the pain will be short-lived. Let's not wait around to find out. Just punch it!'

'Give me a moment.' Ella closed her eyes and took a deep breath.

'A moment?' Anaïs squirmed in her seat. 'We don't have a moment.'

'You know we have absolutely no idea where we're going to end up?' said Ella.

'I get that. Personally, I'm used to it. It's nothing new to me. I never know where I'm going to end up. I've said it before: go with the flow. Or? Do we have another choice?'

'No,' said Ella. 'We don't. And you're right. If we're going with the flow I prefer a flow of compressed air to one of molten lava. Are you strapped in?'

'Oh, no,' said Anaïs, slightly embarrassed by her forgetfulness. *You idiot! Get it together.* She fastened her harness and tugged down on the bindings. 'Okay, done!'

Ella raised her arm and gave a thumbs-up. She interlocked her fingers and flexed them. Her knuckles cracked. She wiggled her digits to loosen them and began punching buttons on the console. The thump of pumps and hiss of compressed air filled the tube, drowning out all sounds of the eruption outside. The air pressure dropped. Anaïs grabbed her nose. With her mouth closed she filled her cheeks and popped her eardrums to equalise the pressure.

'Here goes nothing,' muttered Ella to herself. She twisted a lever and pressed more buttons. The vehicle began to whine and shudder. Using the chrome automotive lever in her armrest, Ella released the brakes.

The force of the ancient shuttle shooting forward

snapped the little witch's head back against the seat. The acceleration intensified, taking Anaïs's breath away. This tube was much faster than previous one. The vehicle shook as if it were in the process of falling apart. She heard the metal capsule grinding against the outer tube, interrupted only by the occasional clang as it made full contact with the sides. The rattling shook every bone in her body.

The speed continued to increase, pushing her deeper in her seat. Closing her eyes, Anaïs fought to control the bile rising in her throat.

She squeezed the promptuary tightly. A final thought shot through her head before she succumbed to the g-forces and passed out. *Keep us safe.*

On the surface the cacophony from Mount Etna was tremendous. It roared and snorted. Jets of smoke shot miles into the air. As did rocks and boulders of all sizes. Some landed harmlessly in fields. Others rained down on the city, levelling more buildings in the process.

Then came the lava. Several streams of it snaked their way down the steep, snow-capped slopes. The bright orange tentacles, slicing their way through the pure whiteness, were a sight to behold.

Eruptions from Etna were not new to the population. It was a regular occurrence. However, this level of ferocity was unusual. It took the authorities by surprise. Fortunately, years of preparations for such an event kept the casualties to a minimum. Most people had cleared the streets and taken shelter at the beginning of the onslaught.

However, the scale of the destruction this eruption left in its wake would be remembered for years. For a certain little witch the memories would last a good deal longer.

CHANGE

Change is something all of us are confronted with. How we deal with it is a very individual thing.

For some of us change is welcomed with open arms. We relish every fresh challenge and grasp the chance for a new beginning with both hands. For others, it is a mountain so high it is impossible to climb. It is a wall, a barrier, where the mere idea of having to overcome it is insurmountable.

Witches fall into the first group. Even worse, they have no choice in the matter. They have to go on, no matter what the obstacle. Admittedly they have magic on their side. However, magic will never be enough unless it is backed up with the will to succeed.

This will is instilled in witches from an early age. From the very beginning they are forced to travel light, move at a moment's notice, or uproot and leave everything behind. Being a witch means you are constantly confronted with the unknown—in particular an unknown future.

Staying put attracts unwanted attention. Practising their unusual exploits would be impossible if they were constantly scrutinised. It is far better to fly in, do the job, and get out fast—ideally, without being seen. This is not always possible. There are solutions. However, flushing people's memories is complicated, and time consuming. A better option is to do your thing and be gone in a wink of an eye.

If a little bit of magic is noticed and then the cause of it disappears, naturals are usually able to cope. They will question what they have seen. Possibly even investigate. Upon finding nothing concrete, they will wonder what just happened. The rest will be left up to their imagination to play havoc with them—a magical force unto itself.

A life as a nomad is what lies before a witch. A life of constant change.

Anaïs struggled with this. She, like many of us, would have preferred to run away and hide from confrontation—turn a blind eye to the challenge—yet this was impossible. The deeper she became ensconced in the witch world, the further she travelled from the possibility of ever escaping her tasks.

Deep down she knew this already. Even if she was unwilling to admit it. Proclaiming 'Go with the flow' demonstrated this. She knew she was stuck in flux. What she had was a job for life. She could never contemplate going on holiday. This would probably not bother her anyway. She was certainly not one to curl up on a towel on the beach and read a good book. She had to be content with her experiences as a form of relief. To try to approach them as entertainment. For her, change was the norm. Change was the holiday.

It would always dog her. Adaptability was par for the course. The changes she was confronted with could not be avoided. They would come at any moment and usually did on an all-too-regular basis.

The only respite she was ever likely to receive came when she slept. And that happened as rarely as going on vacation occurs for many naturals. Unfortunately, with it came the added complication of not knowing what would happen to her in her sleep. Most of us enjoy slumber when we can get it. For her it was no holiday. For her it signalled the grandmother of all changes.

As a natural you are fortunate. You will have respite. Although change is inevitable, you will usually see it coming your way. You will have an inkling of when it will occur. You will have the luxury to prepare for it. So, when it arrives, seize it with all you've got. The mountains you will have to climb are nothing compared to those facing Anaïs.

Remain eternally thankful that you have some kind of control over change. As a witch, change controls you.

LAVA

Caput Mortuum's face was a twisted ball of rage. 'What's wrong with you? Can't you get anything right? She's dangerous. Why didn't you put a stop to her?'

'But—'

'But nothing!' screamed the witch. 'It's not good enough!'

'I didn't have the dogs,' protested the Inquisitor. 'What was I supposed to do?'

Caput sneered at him. 'You have your promptuary. Use that!'

'I did, but she has one too.'

'She's young—a novice. She doesn't know how to use it properly.'

'Be that as it may, she seemed to do pretty well with it.' Now it was Ignatius who simmered with rage. 'Anyway! It was your fault. You distracted me.'

'I didn't expect her to do what she did. Did I?'

'Still.' He hunched his shoulders. 'You can't dump

all the blame on me. You had a hand in it too. Now we're stuck cleaning up her mess.'

Mother and son ducked instinctively as a fresh shower of stones pelted them. Protective shields, created by their handbooks, surrounded them in impenetrable bubbles. The stones bounced harmlessly off the force fields.

Caput dismissed his comment with a wave of her hand. 'It was a ploy. I was trying to draw her in. I thought if you were out of the picture, she would come to me. I was also concerned about your sister. Besides, I can't help it that Anaïs is so unpredictable.'

The Inquisitor scowled. 'That's another thing. It might have helped if someone had filled me in about Nan.'

'You mean your father never told you about her?'

'No!' Ignatius retorted angrily. 'Why would I do any of this if I knew otherwise? She's my sister, for Pete's sake. I thought she was just a worthless shade. I didn't recognise her in her camouflage. Besides, Nan is not her real name anyway. How was I supposed to know?'

He drew his palm over his polished skull, removing a layer of sweat. He shook his hand, flicking the perspiration aside. It splashed against the inside of the protective sphere, hissing on contact.

'You're not free from guilt either,' he continued, glaring at his mother. 'You could have told me about her. I trusted you. You and Dad are as bad as one another.'

Caput Mortuum opened her mouth to defend herself.

Sighing, he cut her off. 'Forget it. We can't do much about it now. We have to fix this.' He looked around him. 'What a mess!' Lava flowed around his protective sphere. Had it not been there, he would have stood knee-deep in the boiling fluid. 'What's the plan here, anyway?'

Caput looked down the mountain. 'Try to redirect this so it doesn't hit the city.'

Ignatius swung his arm towards the mountain's summit. 'What about sealing the crater?'

'No, her blocking it was what caused this in the first place,' replied Caput. 'The best we can do is let it run its course.'

'Its course? We can't be everywhere at once!'

'I'm well aware of that,' said Caput. 'Help is on its way.'

'Well, it better hurry up!'

'Patience.' The witch flared her nostrils. 'Really! You're just like your father. Where is he anyway?'

Trickles of sweat ran from his temples. Ignatius wiped his sleeve across his brow. 'No idea.'

'Useless!'

He shrugged. 'Maybe he went after her.'

'I'm surprised you men can get anything together. Don't you communicate?'

'Of course we do!' retorted the Inquisitor. 'But this is an emergency. Nobody saw it coming. Not even you. You just said that.'

Caput relented. 'Okay, you have a point.' She shook her head. 'I still can't believe he never told you about Nan.'

'Nobody tells me anything!' he yelled, infuriated. 'The two of you never talk. You leave it up to me. I'm sick of being your go-between. You need to bury your differences.'

'You know that's never going to happen, Ignatius,' said Caput quietly.

'Stop calling me that. You know I prefer Iggy.'

'It's the name I gave you. Just accept it. Your friends can call you that.'

'Friends? What friends?' exclaimed Iggy, his face turning red. 'Where the hell am I going to find friends with the crap I have to do?'

'We all have the same problem. Why was your sister even in the crater?'

'Insurance,' said Iggy. 'In case Anaïs turned up while I was getting a hound. Which she did.'

'Well, that strategy really panned out, didn't it?'

'No.' He bowed his head in dismay. 'Knowing what I know now, I honestly can't believe he would stoop so low as to use her like that.'

'It doesn't surprise me,' said Caput, curling her lip. 'Let's sort this out first.'

A surge of lava hit her protective dome. It gushed up the side and cascaded over the top of it. She flinched, crouching and sheltering her head. She watched the surge ebb and the remnants of it drip down the sides of the dome.

Regaining her composure, Caput stood. She spoke sternly. 'We can discuss her later.'

Iggy rubbed his slick skull again, letting out a loud

puff of air. He flicked his thumb over his shoulder. 'Fine. I'll go this way and you the other. Okay?'

Caput nodded. 'Okay.'

Heading in opposite directions the two witches separated. Using the power of their spheres they waded through the deep streams of lava, slicing horizontal furrows around the mountain. The intense flow of lava hampered their progress, making the going slow. Often they were completely submerged, the rivers of molten rock crashing in waves over their protective spheres.

~

From a helicopter circling above the volcano, the pilot noted the lava flow's sudden change in direction. He radioed it in to emergency crews working at the foot of the mountain, carving their own furrows through the earth with excavators.

Peering through binoculars he inspected the course of the lava closely. He could see what appeared to be balls of fire creating two new streams. He shook his head in disconcertion. He swore he saw shadowy human shapes within the balls.

Impossible! People can't walk in rivers of fire.

He screwed up his nose and squinted. He inspected the flow again. He smiled, reassuring himself that what he saw were merely clumps of blackened rock in the stream playing tricks with his eyes.

PHYSICAL DYSFUNCTION

Something was not right. Anaïs felt different. Something had changed. Even before she opened her eyes she knew it. It started with her hand.

She pulled it out from beneath the sheets and held it in front of her face. Cautiously, she peered out between her lids. She didn't dare fully open her eyes for fear of what she would see. Eventually, she relented and assessed her hand.

Something had definitely changed. Her hand was bigger.

Her palm had creases in it which had not been there before. Three distinct lines carved their way across it. One ran horizontally from the middle of her palm to above her thumb. Two others ran from the edges of this line down to her wrist. Together they formed a perfect triangle. They were etched deep into the skin, as if they had been there for years. Small furrows fanned out from the main lines like cracks in shattered safety glass. Her fingers were longer, slender and thin, not short, fat and stumpy.

She turned her palm away from her and examined her knuckles. The skin was no longer pulled tightly across them; it bagged up slightly as she flexed her fingers and straightened them. Her fingernails were also longer. They had a strange sheen to them and were finely manicured, terminating in a sharp point. They looked stronger yet more brittle, not soft and malleable as they had been.

She exhaled softly, feeling the warmth of her own breath on her skin. If she had any doubts about the hand really being her own they were put to rest. She closed her eyes and tensed the quadriceps in her legs. They felt more muscular. She wiggled her toes and stretched them. They were not under the covers and were exposed and cold. She shuddered. She could feel the soft edge of the weight of her bedding cutting across her legs just below the knee. More than the feather weight she felt a definite line between warmth and cold where the bedding touched her skin.

She slid her hand under the covers and ran it down the length of her body. She was wearing some kind of skin-tight material. It felt weird, like a body suit. It hugged her upper body. Her arm seem to stretch out forever. She could reach her knees with her fingertips.

Had that been possible before?

She drew her hand up over her torso. She encountered strange forms on her chest. There were soft bumps which hadn't been there before. She could no longer feel the sharp solidity of her ribcage. There was a lot more padding between skin and bone. She changed direction and ran her hands back down across her stomach. It was soft like a pillow. Beneath her taut, thin clothing there was a mound of something coarse and wire-like covering her crotch. She stopped.

'Aaaaaah-ie!'

Anaïs threw off the covers and sprang out of bed. The floor was a lot closer than she expected. Jarring her ankles on it, she cried out with a yelp. She had intended to jump down from the bed and not stand up from it. The small distance to the floor failed to enable her to stretch her legs fully. She fell forward and slid down onto her hands and knees.

She stopped, staring at the wooden floorboards under her hands. They were old and dark brown. Dust and grime filled the gaps between the boards. Then she lifted her head slightly. She was not alone. Two bare feet greeted her. She sucked in her breath.

'Anaïs? Are you okay?'

She exhaled with relief. The voice was familiar. 'I don't know,' she replied. She raised her eyes to meet Nan's. 'I don't think so.'

'You grew again.'

'I gathered that.' Anaïs frowned. 'I'm a little afraid to know how much, though.'

The caretaker's eyes roved over her. *'My guess is you are physically now eleven or twelve years old. But it's a bit hard to tell with you on all fours on the floor.'*

Anaïs climbed to her feet. She dusted off her knees. Knees which were now knobbly. *Damn! I liked my old body.* She looked around the room. It was small and filled with antique furniture. Not only the floorboards, but everything in it was brown. 'Where are we?'

'Venice.'

'Venice?'

'Yes'

'Wow! How did I get here?'

'Here? Venice you mean?'

'No, I get the Venice bit, I think,' said Anaïs. *So that's where the tube went.* She pointed at the floor. 'I mean here.'

'You passed out in the tube. We brought you up to this room and put you to bed.'

Anaïs moved to the window. She peered out through the smudged glass. They were on a narrow canal. High water lapped over the stone pathways which lined it, and almost up to the entrances of houses. Below her, a number of people filed along raised narrow duckboards which had been put in place on the pathways to allow passage over the water. 'How long have I been out?'

'A few days.'

Anaïs shrugged. 'Better than the last time this happened, I suppose. I was out for a week then.' She turned away from the window. 'Where are the others?'

'Downstairs. We are above an Apotheek. Below it is the tube junction. From what we can tell it's been abandoned for a while. Ella has been trying to figure it out.'

'So, we are safe?' said Anaïs. 'Safe from them?'

'Them?'

'The Ethnarch and his honchos.'

'Honchos?' Nan's eyes sparkled. Clearly she was smiling beneath her camouflage.

Anaïs smiled in return. 'You know what I mean.'

Nan batted her lids. *'Yes, we're safe. But I doubt it will remain that way. They will be looking for you.'*

'They're always looking for me.' She glanced down at her feet and grimaced. *Man! Look at those toes!* She paused, considering the rest of her body. *Too many changes. Wait! Isn't that a good thing?* She brightened and raised her eyes to meet those of her caretaker across the room. 'Maybe looking like this will make it more difficult for them?'

'I wouldn't count on it. It hasn't stopped them before.'

'Mm …' Anaïs pursed her lips and sighed. 'Do you know anything about Sicily and the volcano?'

'It has been pretty devastating, but the eruption seems to have slowed.'

Anaïs paled and sniffed. 'All those people. What have I done?'

Nan moved across the room. She laid a cold hand on the witch's shoulder. She shivered. *'It wasn't your fault, Anaïs. You did what you thought necessary under the circumstances. They forced your hand. They caused this. Not you.'*

'I should have been more careful. I just … just,' Anaïs stuttered. 'I didn't know. I didn't know I could even do what I did.'

'You used your instincts,' said Nan softly. *'There's nothing wrong with that. Nobody really knows what they're capable of until they try.'*

Anaïs groaned. 'I certainly know now.'

'Yes, you do.' The shade's eyes glinted. *'It's all experience, Anaïs. Take it with you, and next time—if there is a next time—you'll know how to make better use of your powers.'*

The witch's stomach rumbled loudly.

'We can talk about this later. You must be starving. All that growing costs a lot of energy. Let's get some food into you.'

Anaïs nodded. Nan led the way to the door. Anaïs followed slowly. She moved tentatively, feeling unstable on her new legs. 'We better take it easy.' She stopped and hopped from one leg to the other, flexing her ankles. It made her dizzy and she grabbed the chest of drawers next to the door for support. She indicated her legs. 'I have to get used to these things.'

Nan chuckled. *'I fully understand, but I'm here to help. As I always am, Anaïs.'*

The witch steadied herself. 'I know. Thank you for reminding me, Nan. I couldn't do it without you.'

'No need to thank me, Anaïs.' The caretaker placed a cold but reassuring hand on the witch's shoulder. *'That's what big sisters are for.'*

FOUNTAIN OF YOUTH

Witch or no witch, we are all lumbered with a physical form we have no control over. Eventually, we do gain control over it and, unfortunately at some point, we also lose that control, but we never have a say in the form we are given.

I caught my reflection in the mirror the other day and I have to say that what I saw … Well, perhaps some things are better left unspoken.

The physical predicament of witches goes to the extreme. For some, I suppose, having a body which ages slowly may be considered fortunate, although it does present a whole set of other challenges.

Many of us would relish the opportunity to hold onto our youth. If we set aside people with the finances to augment their appearance, most naturals suffer the opposite: the body degrades whilst the mind remains relatively young. Some mentally never get out of puberty. Often it is only when we truly know the world around us that we have the opportunity to enjoy our youthfulness. At which point, if we exercise it in a youthful way, we are looked down upon by our peers for behaving like children and not acting our age.

This attitude is unfortunate, as nurturing our inner child has a positive effect on longevity. The ability to go out and entertain oneself, in a playground of choice, relieves stress and makes life all the more enjoyable. How can that be a bad thing? I'm no scientist, but happiness is surely an antidote for ageing.

Anaïs was stuck somewhere in between. Apart from her physical disability—her Lilliputian size—she had the knowledge and experience of someone far beyond her mental years.

Not everyone is forced to travel the world chasing demons, or has to solve the mysteries of shades who have an entire lifetime behind them. Even though she'd had less than twenty years on the planet to learn the ropes, she was certainly no teenager in the normal sense. It's actually a miracle that she copes with it all in the fashion she does. I, for one, would be tearing my hair out. But then, witches are obviously also blessed with an ironclad mental constitution to fortify them against this sort of thing.

It may be that naturals have more in common with witches than they imagine. We may even have a distinct advantage over them. For if we can maintain some form of innocence, and the attitude of a child, we can stretch our time.

We don't have to deal with demons, except perhaps personal ones. In most cases, with a bit of effort, they can be exorcised. We don't have to help others solve their unfinished business. Especially not those who have gone before they can solve it. We only have to finish our own.

Be thankful for your lot. You are not saddled with the witch problem of a youthful exterior and an aged mental capacity. There are advantages to being in the opposite state.

As a natural, count yourself lucky. Your fountain of youth exists on the inside.

FRUSTRATION

Anaïs looked at her empty plate. She felt full—satisfied—yet strangely empty.

She studied her new hands again. She examined the triangular shape on her palm. Recalling the burn mark she picked up from Marilyn's compact on Malta, she realised it had completely disappeared. Ella's salve had done its work well.

She turned her hands around in front of her face. The lines on the back of them were many—fine, criss-crossing all over the place. The skin there seemed have aged faster than the rest of her body.

She snorted loudly and slammed her fists down on the table.

'What did I do to deserve this?' she yelled.

The witch's outburst snapped Nan out of her listless state. *'Wha— What do you mean?'*

Anaïs slapped her breast twice with both hands. 'This! This stupid body. Why is this only happening to me?'

'It's not only you. It happens to all of us, Anaïs. We all age. Only in different ways. We don't always get to be what we want to be.' Nan fell silent for a moment. She stared at the table. *'I didn't choose to be this, but I have to accept it.'*

'I know,' said Anaïs with a pained expression. 'That wasn't your fault, though. I made you this way.'

'No, you're wrong. You didn't make *me anything, Anaïs.'*

'But—'

'No buts!' snapped the caretaker, slightly irritated. She took a moment to calm herself before continuing. *'I told you before. None of this is your fault. We are what we are. We are what we become. We have to accept that and be ourselves. Every one of us is special in our own way. We are all individuals. That's a good thing.'*

'How can this be a good thing?' The little witch gesticulated at herself. 'I keep changing.'

'No, you don't. Not everywhere.' Nan tapped her temple. *'You are what you are on the inside, Anaïs. Not what others see on the outside. That won't change. That is important. No matter what happens, no one can take that away from you.'*

'I don't believe that.' Anaïs shook her head vigorously. 'The Organisation want me to be a certain way. My father wanted me to do it his way. I only get criticism for what I do.'

'That may be so, but I don't see you paying much attention to them. When have you ever done what they wanted?'

Anaïs slumped in her seat. She ran her hands over her knees and stared at them. 'Okay, you've got a point.'

'Stay true to yourself, Anaïs,' said Nan. *'No one can take that away from you.'* She bent forward to draw the witch's attention. Anaïs raised her head. Their eyes met. *'It*

doesn't mean you can do whatever you want to do. But that is not in your nature anyway. I haven't seen you doing that. I've only seen you do what you think to be right. And you've done a pretty good job at it, considering how much knowledge you have.'

'Then I guess I need more knowledge,' said Anaïs. 'I need more experience.'

'Yes, and you will get it. You only have to learn not to be so impatient. It will all come in time.'

'That's frustrating as hell.'

Nan chuckled. *'If there is such a thing as hell, I'm certain the part about it being frustrating will be the least of your problems.'*

Anaïs smiled. 'Going on my level of frustration, I think we're there already.' She rubbed her palms together and opened them. She studied the weird lines and frowned. 'Maybe there is someone who can help.'

'I'm sure there is.'

'Perhaps Sojourner Pink,' said Anaïs. 'You remember her? Immi and Hank's mother. She helped before in Barcelona.' Anaïs stared at the empty plate in front of her. 'Anyone's better than your mother. I don't trust her.'

'I don't either, but that's personal.'

'I don't think not trusting her has anything to do with how well you know her, Nan. I hardly know the woman and she's never given me a reason to trust her. She's never really helped. Sojourner, on the other hand, has. I wish I knew how to contact her.'

'I wouldn't worry about that now,' said Nan. *'Witches always turn up of their own accord. They have a habit of doing that for some reason. I think it's better we keep doing what we're*

doing for now and keep a low profile. We're safe here. The right help will come. Someone will find us eventually.'

'I don't doubt that.' The little witch sighed. 'I certainly hope it is the right help, though.' She considered her options for a moment. She looked Nan in the eye. 'Okay, you're right. We have no choice I suppose. Let's wait. Any idea what to do until the cavalry arrives?'

Anaïs sensed Nan shrugging. *'Do what we always did.'*

'What's that?'

'When all else fails, go shopping.'

'Shopping?'

'Yeah, you need new clothes. You grew. Or have you forgotten already?'

Anaïs smirked. She looked at what was left of the pyjamas she wore. They were at least two sizes too small and hugged her body. The hems on her pyjama legs had split. 'No forgetting that,' she murmured. 'I now know how the Incredible Hulk must feel.'

Nan laughed. *'Just be thankful you haven't turned green as well.'*

Anaïs grinned broadly and nodded in agreement.

'Well then,' said Nan. *'Let's take advantage of the situation. Milan would probably be a better place to get the latest fashion, but I'm sure Venice is a worthy alternative.'*

'Okay!' cried Anaïs. She pushed her chair back from the table and stood. The hems on her arms and legs let out a loud ripping sound as they tore further. She ignored them. 'What are we waiting for. Let's hit the streets!'

ATTITUDE ADJUSTMENT

Downstairs in the cellar, Ella was tinkering away at a table in what appeared to be an abandoned apotheek. Engrossed in her work, she did not look up when they entered.

Moisture-laden, the room had the overpowering stale odour of disuse. Much smaller than the other apotheeks she had been in, it had a ceiling low enough for Anaïs to almost reach. She glanced around the room. The walls and ceiling were covered in dark oak panelling. A large set of small drawers dominated one wall. Many of them were open. They lacked the usual signal lights found on the face of drawers in other apotheeks. As far as Anaïs could see, the drawers themselves were empty. It appeared the place had been deserted in a hurry. She took reassurance in the fact that, for the moment, they would be safe from the prying eyes of other witches.

'We're going out for a bit,' said Anaïs.

'Um … Okay. See you when you get back.' Ella

stopped what she was doing. ‘Oh good, you’re awake.’ She looked up from her magnifying glass and callipers. Her jaw dropped. ‘Whoa! What happened to you?’

‘I grew,’ said Anaïs flatly.

‘That’s obvious.’ The Apothecary stared wide-eyed at the little witch. ‘If I hadn’t heard your voice first I’d have thought you were a total stranger.’

‘C’mon,’ said Anaïs, cracking a weak smile, ‘I don’t look that different.’

‘Well, no. But different enough.’ Ella dropped her callipers on the workbench. She scratched her head. ‘Think I’m gonna need a minute to process this.’

‘Take all the time in the world.’

‘How did this happen?’

‘No idea. A witch thing. It happened to me once before. The weird thing is it never used to happen, but recently—every time I sleep—I wake up older.’

‘We all have that problem,’ joked Ella. ‘Although, I have to say this is pretty extreme. One more reason not to be a witch.’

‘Yep.’

‘How does it feel?’

‘Weird,’ said Anaïs, twisting her lip. ‘Kind of having trouble with my balance. And there’s these.’ She waved at her breasts.

‘So I see. Same problem here.’ She indicated her own chest. ‘A woman’s curse.’

‘I hope not. Guess I’ll just have to get used to them.’

‘It helps if you pack them in. Especially if you’re going to do some running.’

‘Running! I can barely walk properly.’

'Like I said, a woman's curse,' said Ella. She eyed Anaïs's clothing. 'I think you need a whole new wardrobe,'

'That's the plan.' Anaïs nodded at her caretaker. 'We're going shopping.'

Nan had done her best to find suitable attire. She had combined the clothes Anaïs had been wearing on the trip from Sicily with the limited resources in the house. Everything was a tight fit. Her sleeves stopped in the middle of her forearms. The pipes of her trousers fit snugly around her legs. Unable to move her limbs freely, Anaïs felt like a robot. To make matters worse, she had to slide her feet across the floor. She wore a pair of oversized rubber gardening boots Nan had found in a cupboard.

Ella stifled a chuckle at her appearance. 'Good idea.'

'You all right here?'

'Of course,' said Ella cheerily. 'Never better.'

'What are you doing?'

'Repairing one of my remotes.'

'What does it do?'

Ella shrugged. 'No idea. That's why I'm fixing it. I told you I had too many of these things.' She peered at the wiring. 'Just hope this isn't the one for my coffee machine on Malta. Gonna be a big mess if that's the case.'

Anaïs grinned. 'Or for your broomstick. Wouldn't want that going off.'

'No,' said Ella, shaking her head. 'That would be a disaster.'

'I'll leave you to it.'

'Have fun!'

'Will do,' chirped the witch.

Nan and Anaïs climbed the narrow staircase and re-entered the kitchen.

'Whoa!'

'Hi Immi,' said Anaïs.

The librarian screwed up her face. 'What happened to you?'

'I grew. You know, like in the train from England.'

'That's obvious.'

'Do I look that bad?'

'No,' said Immi. 'But if this keeps up you'll be taller than I am. I thought witches were supposed to grow slowly.'

'I suppose I'm no ordinary witch.'

Immi nodded. 'Clearly.'

'It wouldn't be hard to be taller than you anyway.'

Nan interjected, laying a cold hand on the librarian's shoulder and giving her a start. She cautioned Anaïs, *'Don't the two of you dare start with this again.'*

Anaïs bit her lip. Sending thoughts back to her caretaker, she offered her apologies.

'No need to say sorry, Anaïs. Just don't do it.'

The witch cleared her throat. 'Where are the others?'

Immi massaged her shoulder. 'Others?'

'The shades.'

'Oh, them,' said Immi nonchalantly. 'They're still strapped in the tube.'

Anaïs's eyes widened. 'What! What are they still doing there?'

'You were asleep.' Immi hunched her shoulders. 'What else were we supposed to do? You're the expert and, besides, I didn't want them running away.'

'Why would they do that?' Anaïs knotted her brow. 'In my experience shades don't do a lot of running around. And even if they did, why would it be a problem?'

'You took them with you, not me,' said Immi defensively. 'I was trying to keep them safe. I assumed you still wanted to help them.'

'Perhaps,' said Anaïs. 'I'm slightly preoccupied with other things. There's an entire world of shades out there to help, Immi. But that will have to come later. At the moment I don't see the problem with losing a couple of them.'

'That's a bit callous.' Immi began to fume. 'I honestly don't know why I bother helping you.'

Anaïs opened her mouth to retort, then thought better of it. Although Immi did not know it, Joan had helped her. Some shades were especially valuable. The librarian had done the right thing. She heeded Nan's earlier advice about not raising Immi's ire. 'Thanks for thinking of me, Immi. And for taking care of them. It's good you kept them in a safe place.'

Surprised by the witch's reaction, the librarian gaped at her. She blubbered, struggling to form words. 'Are … um … Are you feeling okay?'

'Never been better,' said Anaïs a little too cheerfully. 'If you don't mind, I'm going to go for a walk with Nan. I need to adjust to this.' She glanced down at her boots.

Man! They are so far away. 'I'll check on the shades after that.'

'Um … Okay,' said Immi.

Anaïs nudged Nan. She flashed her eyes at the corridor leading off the kitchen. *'Do we go this way?'*

'Ahem, yes,' replied the caretaker, similarly taken aback by the witch's sudden self-restraint and subtle handling of the librarian.

'See you later, Immi,' Anaïs called over her shoulder as she set off down the corridor. She paused to select an overcoat from the hanger next to the front door.

Nan and Immi glanced at each other.

Even though the librarian could not read her face, she sensed that both her and Nan were aligned in recognising Anaïs's sudden turn of maturity. Had Anaïs's growth been more than skin deep?

THE WITCH'S NEW CLOTHES

The witch studied her reflection in the mirror. Her new clothes fit like a glove. *Finally! No more walking around in ill-fitting stuff.* She tugged on the sleeves of her trench coat and extended her arms to check they covered her wrists. *Perfect!* She turned sideways and smoothed the jacket down. Checking her look in the mirror once again, she grinned. *What a fantastic shade of purple.*

She pulled the collar up and drew it snug around her neck. Glancing at Nan, she beamed at the shade. 'I'll take them!'

'Good. I'm glad you're happy. Although, the coat makes you look like Humphrey Bogart.'

'Who?'

'Never mind. Not sure about the riding boots, though.'

'They're cool!' Anaïs lifted one foot and admired the deep purple sheen on the calf-length boots. 'Besides, half the city is under water.'

'I suppose you have a point.'

'I have to think practical here, Nan. We could end up anywhere.'

'Hopefully this will last you a while. If you keep growing like you do, we'll be shopping every week.'

'That's something I don't have a problem with.' Anaïs grinned. 'Bring on the growth. I'm so sick of being treated like a kid.'

'All in good time, Anaïs. You should be glad you've grown this fast. I'm sure other witches don't grow like you.'

'I don't care about them. I'm me.'

'You certainly are. One of a kind. If you're finished, let's get out of here.'

Anaïs nodded. She checked the price tags. 'How are we going to pay for this?' she said, scratching her head. 'Wait. I have an idea. Let me try something.' She produced her promptuary, closed her eyes and concentrated. The handbook emitted a loud 'ker-ching!'. A small wad of euros shot out from between the pages. Anaïs opened her eyes and beamed with delight.

'I wish we'd known about this earlier. It would have saved us a bunch of money.'

Anaïs extracted the notes from the promptuary. 'Well, we know now.'

'That we do.'

They both stepped out of the dressing room and Anaïs led the way to the cashier. She paid her. The cashier suggested she also get a new hat. Anaïs shook her head. 'No thanks. I'm quite attached to my beret.' Surprisingly, it was the only piece of attire which still fitted.

'And your other clothes?' enquired the woman. 'Shall I put them in a bag for you?'

'No, that won't be necessary,' said Anaïs. 'I don't need them any more.'

The cashier shrugged. 'Okay, suit yourself.'

'No, wait,' said Anaïs. 'One moment please.'

She rifled through the pockets of her old clothing. All were empty except one. Out of her jacket pocket she retrieved a small golden ball. She opened her palm and the ball unfurled, revealing itself to be a clump of thread.

'Are you collecting fluff now?' said the caretaker sarcastically.

'Very funny,' said Anaïs, sending out her thoughts to Nan. *'No, I got it in Amalfi. They used this thread to repair my promptuary. Maybe it will come in useful.'*

Anaïs shoved the ball of thread into the pocket of her new jacket. She slid her old clothing across the counter to the cashier. 'Thank you.'

The cashier offered the witch her change. Anaïs waved her hand. 'You keep that too. Thank you for the service.'

'*Prego*. You are too kind. Maybe your grandmother would also like to try something on?'

Anaïs looked at Nan. In her camouflage she swayed listlessly on the spot. 'No, she will be fine. Thank you again.'

'A pleasure,' said the cashier brightly. 'Thank you for the tip.'

'Don't mention it. C'mon, Nan, let's go.'

Together they stepped out of the shop into the crisp

winter air. Anaïs shivered. 'Brrr … I wish I could change the weather.'

'Even if you could, that might be pushing it too far. I think we should stick to keeping a low profile.'

'I guess you're right.' Anaïs looked at the shop front. 'Do you remember the last time we did this?'

'What?'

'Shopping. It was back in Amsterdam.'

'Ah, yes.'

'That was before …' Anaïs stopped herself. She tried to read the caretaker's eyes. They had glazed over. 'Oh, Nan, sorry. Maybe we shouldn't think about that.'

'No.' The caretaker cleared her throat. *'We shouldn't. Let's stick to looking forward. We can't change what happened.'*

Anaïs sniffed. The cold air bit her nostrils, causing her eyes to water.

'Are you all right?'

Anaïs nodded and ran her sleeve under her nose.

'Do you have to do that? It's a new coat.'

'Sorry,' said Anaïs. 'Force of habit. And it's cold.'

'Then let's get back to the house where it's warm. Shall we?'

'Yes,' said Anaïs, taking Nan by the arm. They made their way along the makeshift footbridge. Freezing water lapped over the edges of the wooden planks. The seasonal tide, the *acqua alta*, had flooded large sections of the city.

Reaching a small square, they stepped off the duckboards and up onto stone tiles. Anaïs stopped. A fresh shiver ran up her spine. This one did not come from the cold weather nor the chill from the caretaker's arm. A sense of foreboding came over her.

She looked across the square at a larger building. It appeared to be a church. A screech, like the sound of a nail across a blackboard, pierced the witch's ears.

'Ow!' Anaïs dropped Nan's arm. She cupped her hands over her ears.

'What is it?'

'Did you hear that?'

'Hear what?'

'That sound.'

'The water?'

Anaïs shook her head.

'What then? I don't hear a thing.'

'Stay here, Nan.'

'Sorry?'

'Stay here.' Anaïs pointed across the square. 'There's something in there. I have to check it out. It's somewhere you shouldn't go.'

'I shouldn't go? Then why should you?'

'I don't know. I just have to. Alone. Something tells me it's important. Wait here. I'll be right back.'

Not waiting for a response, Anaïs marched across the square, leaving Nan in her wake. Another, longer screech shot through her skull, punctuated by the panicked call from her caretaker. *'Anaïs! Please be careful!'*

I'll certainly do that, thought the little witch to herself.

THE OLD CHURCH

It was very unchurch-like. No pews, no organ, no pillars supporting the roof. It was a single room, a huge, grand, cavernous space. Empty, except for a wooden-walled area in the centre. This appeared to be an afterthought and stood like a small forested island in a sea of rock. The floor was covered in stone tablets. Not regular stone tiles, but huge slabs of it. All different sizes. Well worn. The floor undulated like waves gently rising and falling on a calm lake. Evidently, thousands of feet had trampled upon it over the years and moulded its shape.

Anaïs walked across the space and looked up at the windows high in the wall. That was another curious thing. The windows were several storeys above her. They ran around the circumference of the room just under the eaves, letting in light but not prying eyes from outside. They did not function as normal windows. Even if it were possible to find a ladder long enough, the frosted glass would prevent anyone seeing out.

The vaulted ceiling had the same construction as the inside of an ancient ship. She tilted her head and, as the windows rotated, she had the impression she was looking at an upended Roman galleon. She envisioned slaves sweating, pounding the oars under the lash of a whip.

The soft light filtering through the windows barely reached her. It failed to fully illuminate the stone beneath her feet. This made crossing the floor precarious. She felt her way across it, tapping her foot in front of her. Gaining confidence, she moved faster across the open space. Then she tripped on the edge of a slab and crashed to her knees. She yelped with pain from the impact.

She rolled over and sat up. Grimacing, she vigorously rubbed the pain from her knees. Now that she was so near to the floor, she could make out more detail. She looked closely at the slabs around her. Some were completely smooth. Some were pockmarked. The etchings in them had worn down to almost nothing. Others clearly had writing on them. Whoever had been responsible for the chiselling had made fastidious work of it. Even the centuries of wear had not made an impression on some of them. She stood and studied the one under her feet. She spread her feet apart and crouched to get a better look. It had a date deeply etched into it—1732.

Then she realised what she was looking at. The slabs of stone were not building blocks. They were tombstones. She peered across the church. It was a graveyard. Only one with horizontal headstones. It was as if they had all been blown flat by a strong wind. She had walked across graves—hundreds of them.

She rubbed her knees again. The pain had now almost completely gone. She stood full-length and arched her back. She took out her promptuary and opened it.

'Reveal,' she commanded.

The pages lit up, flickered and transformed into something akin to a television screen. The image it displayed was not in full colour, more shades of blue and white—an X-ray. Anaïs could see beneath the floor. Holding the book at arm's length she panned it before her as she rotated her body on the spot. The image zoomed in and out. It blurred and then came into focus. It showed her deep under the earth.

A shiver ran down her spine.

She saw bones. Thousands of them. Gleaming white bones. Stacked and layered across one another.

Something caught her eye. She stopped panning. She detected movement. At first it was imperceptible. Then it spread. The bones began to move. In no time, the movement beneath the stones became one seething mass. Tibias and fibulas intertwined. They snaked their way towards each other and began to form entire limbs. Arms slotted into ribcages and reached out for skulls. Skeleton torsos which were relatively intact began to crawl between the loose bones of other more disjointed bodies. They searched for the rest of their skeletal remains. Once connected, entire skeletons began to writhe and roll from side to side, almost as if they were turning over in their sleep.

She let the promptuary drop and panned its camera eye to her feet. Beneath her a fully assembled skeleton with its back to her flipped over. She watched with horror as skin began to regenerate. The empty sockets in its skull suddenly filled. Two eyes emerged. Black spheres narrowed down and white cornea appeared. Two pupils stared straight up at her. Eyelids blinked. The corpse drew back a half-formed arm, and then swept it above its head. It slammed a closed fist on the tombstone beneath her feet. She felt the blow course through the soles of her feet, sending a ripple up her legs. She choked on her breath and slammed the promptuary shut.

The entire floor began to rumble. Hundreds of bony fists pounded the tombstones. The cacophony grew louder. Anaïs dropped the promptuary into her beret. She pulled it over her skull and clapped her hands over her ears.

Her eyes darted frantically around the room. Searching for a way out, she screamed her caretaker's name in earnest and fled to the nearest exit.

Behind her the sharp rapping of bone on rock grew steadily louder. Beneath the flagstones a flood surged towards the surface. A torrent of death began to rise.

SHADE QUAKE

The little witch screamed at the top of her lungs, 'Nan! We have to go! Now!'

Standing outside, with her back to the double doors of the church, she frantically scanned the square. *Where the hell is she?*

'Anaïs?'

The witch glanced to her side. She sighed with relief as the caretaker stepped out from behind a pillar. *Thank goodness!*

'We have to go,' said Anaïs in a harsh whisper.

'I got that. Calm down. What is it?'

'In there …' Anaïs squeaked, gasping for breath.

'What's in there?'

The witch shook her head vigorously. 'You don't want to know.'

'How is not telling me going to help?'

Anaïs clasped her hand to her pounding chest. She paused, waiting a moment for her heartbeat to slow. 'I'll tell you later. Just take my word for it. We have to leave.'

'Leave? Here? Venice? But it's safe here. What have you done?'

'I've done nothing,' said Anaïs quickly, considering if this was true. 'At least I don't think it was me.'

An almighty thump sounded, rocking the large doors on their hinges. Their movement jarred Anaïs in the back. The impact sent her stumbling forward. She regained her balance, whirled around and stared at the doors. Another thump sounded. This time the doors—frames and all—rattled. A fine mist of dust fell from the lintel. To Anaïs's relief the doors themselves remained securely closed.

Nan grabbed Anaïs by the arm. The chill gave her a start. *'What's going on in there?'* The voice in Anaïs's head sounded as if the caretaker was speaking through gritted teeth.

'Nothing good,' replied Anaïs, her voice hushed.

'Well, tell me then. At least give me something.'

'Shades,' hissed Anaïs. 'Lots of them. Can't you hear the noise.'

'Noise? What noise? No. That can't be all there is to it. Shades are everywhere.'

Anaïs eyed the doors. 'Not like this.' A rumbling sent vibrations through the stone underfoot. The racket from within the church of thousands of fists beating the ground grew in volume. 'Nan,' Anaïs pleaded. 'Please! Let's go.'

The vibrations increased. Anaïs felt the earth beneath her lift and sway. She slackened the muscles in her legs to accommodate the movement. She sank through her knees and spread her arms wide for balance, riding the undulation like surfing a wave.

She turned her attention to the shade. Nan seemed unaffected by the movement. The relative calm in her eyes told Anaïs she was unaware of what was going on. 'Nan? Please!'

'What?'

Anaïs hopped from one foot to the other. She pointed at the ground. 'Don't you feel this.'

'I don't feel a thing. Why are you dancing?'

'I'm not dancing.' Her eyes darted back to the doors. They remained shut. She pointed at her feet. 'The ground is moving.'

'Looks like dancing to me.'

'Oh!' Anaïs rolled her eyes. 'Believe me, it's not. We have to go.'

'Fine. Then we go.'

Anaïs grabbed the shade's cold hand. Resisting the urge to shiver, she charged across the square with Nan in tow.

'Hold on. Slow down. Take it easy.'

'No. No time to waste.' Anaïs jumped down onto the wooden boards and shuffled swiftly along them.

'Careful, Anaïs. We don't want to fall in.'

'That's the least of our worries.'

'I still don't get it. What's gotten into you?'

'I said I'll tell you later.' She glanced at the water next to the planks. She noted a ripple. It generated into waves with small peaks until the water was a churning mass, not unlike a spa bath.

Nan saw it too. *'That's strange.'*

'Not as strange as what I just saw.'

'Why won't you tell me?'

'Not now!'

'Sheesh!'

The duckboards ended. Anaïs did not slow. She sprang from the makeshift walkway onto a bridge. She scooted up its steep incline to the highest point. The entire structure began to shake. Anaïs nearly lost her footing on the wet cobblestones. She grabbed the handrail for support. From her elevated viewpoint she could see further down the canal. At the end was the square with the church.

A flock of jackdaws flew from the roof. Circling above the church the small crows formed an ominous cloud. Above them the sky darkened. The entire building began to shake. Small chunks of stonework fell from the eaves. They crashed loudly down into the square.

A flash of lightning lit up the sky, followed by a deep roll of thunder. Large heavy raindrops fell. The heavens opened, dousing Anaïs in torrential rain. She pulled her collar up around her ears.

'Great! That as well!' she exclaimed, wiping water from her face. 'Nan! Let's keep moving!'

She picked her way carefully down the slippery bridge. She jumped onto the boardwalk at the bottom. Peppered with rain, the canal water boiled around it, lapping over the boards. She now stood ankle deep in it. She reached back and grabbed Nan's hand as she stepped down beside her.

Wordlessly, Anaïs led the way, guiding the shade. She

swished through the water, thankful that she had invested in waterproof boots and the trench coat. It was slow going. She stopped.

'Where's the house, Nan?'

'You're going in the right direction. Just down the end of this canal.'

'Good. I totally lost my bearings.' Frantically keeping an eye on the rising water, she continued along the duckboards until they stood before the door to the house. From inside she heard the panicked cries of the Apothecary.

Anaïs paled. 'Oh no, what now?'

DESTINATION UNKNOWN

Unusually for the mild-mannered Apothecary, Ella was beside herself. 'Anaïs, where have you been?'

The witch frowned. 'I told you we were going shopping.'

'Oh, yeah.' Ella ran her hand through her hair. 'I forgot. You know, sometimes I get so totally absorbed in what I'm doing I practically forget my own name.'

Anaïs laughed. 'I can relate to that. Next time I'll double-check with you.'

'Yes, that might help,' said Ella. 'But enough about that. We have a problem.'

'We? I thought it was only me.'

Ella raised an eyebrow. 'What's your problem?'

'Shades.'

'Who? Oh, your ghost thing. Can't help you there,' said Ella. 'That's not my department. You told me you were responsible for them.'

'I am,' Anaïs agreed. 'But this problem is bigger than I can deal with alone. At least I think so.'

'Well,' said Ella. 'Maybe you should get some help.'

'Easier said than done,' said Anaïs and gnawed nervously on her lower lip.

'Why not contact the Organisation?' ventured Ella. 'Isn't that why you have an organisation in the first place?'

Anaïs shrugged. 'I suppose so. I would, but I don't know who I can trust.'

'That *is* a problem.'

'And what's your problem?'

'It's not specifically my problem,' said Ella. 'Somebody was just here and told us we may have to evacuate the city. At any rate, that's what I understood. My Italian is not that good.'

'Why?'

'They're predicting a big earthquake. Didn't you feel the tremors?'

Anaïs cleared her throat. She glanced around the room furtively. 'Oh, that was what that was.' She directed her attention to her caretaker. *'Nan?'*

'Yes Anaïs?'

'I think I *am the problem.'*

'What do you mean?'

'The shades know I'm a witch. Not always, but they usually do.' Anaïs rubbed her chin thoughtfully. *'The penny just dropped. When I get close to the dead, they wake. On Sicily it happened. And now here as well.'*

'Is that what happened back at the church?'

'Yes,' said Anaïs grimly. *'The only thing I don't get is why*

the buried, who have presumably finished their business, are suddenly turning into shades. Well perhaps they're not turning into shades. Who knows? At any rate the dead are waking up.'

'I don't have an answer for you. I'm just happy I'm not one of the dead.'

'Me too. Well, technically you are. But—' Frustrated, she waved her hands next to her head, slapped them on her face and rubbed it vigorously. '*Oh! This is so confusing.'*

'Anaïs, just try to calm down. You'll work it out. What do you want to do about them?'

The little witch took a deep breath and exhaled loudly through her nostrils. *'If I'm the cause, then I have to get away. Go somewhere where there are no dead whatsoever. Somewhere I can't affect them.'*

'That might be difficult. They're everywhere.'

'A desert island, perhaps. I once toyed with the idea back at the port in Naples.' Anaïs glanced up at the caretaker's face sheepishly. *'I have to come clean, Nan. When we were there I nearly ran away.'* She drew her thumb and index finger together, indicating a small gap. *'I came this close to leaving you in the lurch.'*

'When?'

'When he had you trapped on the ship with the dogs. It all got a bit much for me.'

The shade's eye's softened. *'I don't blame you for wanting to run, Anaïs. If it was the other way around I would have wanted to do the same thing.'*

'But I didn't. I was confused—didn't know what to do. I could never leave you, Nan.'

'I know.' Nan laid an icy arm on the witch's

shoulders. Anaïs fought the urge to shiver. *'And thank you for coming back.'*

'Problem is,' said Anaïs, *'I'm in the same quandary now. I don't know what to do.'*

'Do what you always do.'

'What's that?'

'Consult your handbook.'

Anaïs stepped out from under the caretaker's arm. She massaged warmth back into her shoulders and grinned. *'You always know best.'*

'No, not always, but it seems pretty obvious to me.'

Anaïs dropped her gaze to the floor. *'Things always appear a lot more obvious when you're not sitting smack-bang in the middle of them.'*

'Can't argue with that.'

'Were we arguing?'

'Ahem … no,' said Nan, puzzled.

Anaïs nudged the shade. *'Just joking.'*

Nan flashed her eyes. *'Sometimes I can't fathom you.'*

'Sorry, guess I have a weird sense of humour.'

'To be honest that's not the only thing weird about you.' Nan chuckled. *'Ha! There, I did it too.'*

'Anaïs?'

The little witch turned to face the Apothecary. 'Sorry, Ella, I forgot you were there.'

The Apothecary shuffled her feet nervously. 'I don't think we have a lot of time. We need to hurry. If what they said about an earthquake is true, we should get out of here.' She glanced up at the ancient wooden beams supporting the ceiling. 'I'm pretty sure this place is not earthquake-proof.'

'I got that. But the question is: where?' She paused to clear her head. 'Hold on. Give me a moment, will you.' Anaïs retrieved her promptuary. She opened the handbook. Staring blankly at the pages, she scratched her forehead. 'I have no idea what to ask.'

'You said you wanted to get away from shades,' said Nan. *'Start with that.'*

Anaïs raised her eyebrows in delight. 'Good idea!'

'What? What's a good idea?' questioned the Apothecary in confusion.

'Oh. Um … this. This is a good idea.' Anaïs indicated her handbook. 'The promptuary will tell us.' She focussed on the book. *Can you even tell me this?* Sending out her thoughts, she commanded it to show her the whereabouts and concentration of the immediate shade population.

A cloud of glistening dust particles rose from the promptuary's open pages. They whirled in a circular motion. The particles joined together. Solidifying into a sphere they produced a holographic image. It displayed Venice and its surrounding lagoon. A small island near the city was covered beneath a large red dot. It appeared to throb.

'Wow!' exclaimed Anaïs. 'It's busy there. What is that?'

'Busy?' said Ella. 'I doubt it's busy. That's Venice's cemetery. San Michele.'

Anaïs frowned. 'What is it with all these places named after that guy?'

'Sorry? What guy?'

'Oh, never mind. Probably not important. I just

seem to keep hitting spots with his name all over the place.'

'You've been to that cemetery before?'

'No, but I've been to other islands with that name—England, France, and now here. Strange. Who is this Saint Michael anyway?'

Ella thought for a moment. 'From memory I think he was the leader of the armies of good against evil.'

Anaïs snorted and grinned. 'Then I could use his help right now.' She directed her attention to the promptuary. 'Zoom out,' she said. The handbook displayed the surrounding Mediterranean. 'Man! They're everywhere!'

'Who? What?'

'It doesn't matter, Ella. Help me look.' She stared at the image. 'Can you see something without a red dot?'

The Apothecary studied the map. She walked around it and then raised her forefinger and pointed at an island far south and to the east of Venice. 'There.'

'Where is that?'

Ella twisted her lips. 'Somewhere in Greece, I think.'

'Then, Ella, it looks like we are going to Greece.'

The Apothecary brightened. 'Great! I can work on my tan.'

Anaïs frowned. 'It's the middle of winter.'

'No matter.' Ella glanced out the window at the icy rain. 'There has to be more sun there than here.'

'You have a point. Let's get going then,' said Anaïs. 'Oh … but wait. How?'

'I have a solution,' said Ella.

'Every time you say that you make my day.' Anaïs

grinned. 'You don't know how glad I am to have met you, Ella. You always have a solution.'

Ella winked at the witch. 'One day I might not have one. But today is your lucky day. You won't believe what I've found.'

THE WORLD SHIFTS

At first its origins were small. Initially, signs began in Western Europe.

Most naturals noticed it as minor earth tremors. They sensed the occasional rumbling of the ground beneath their feet. In the bigger cities many assumed it was the passing of an underground railway, or a nearby tram or another heavy vehicle. There is so much noise in a city with construction and whatnot that the odd extra sound of thumping could easily be explained. By many city dwellers it went unnoticed, falling on ears deaf to small noises through years of conditioning.

In the silence of the countryside it was a different matter. Why would there be a strange knocking sound coming from the graveyard perched on the hill? Most cast it off as the echo of farm machinery carried on the wind. The more inquisitive went to investigate, but the source of the sounds could not be determined. They were too intermittent to pinpoint.

Yet those in the natural world who did hear it sensed something was afoot. A change had occurred.

Others started seeing things they could not explain. Those with younger and more open minds saw it first. A group of secondary school students visiting Père Lachaise Cemetery in Paris had quite a shock. Hanging around in the crowd surrounding his own grave, the deceased singer of the rock group The Doors—Jim Morrison—dropped his camouflage for an instant. He exposed his true self beneath the mask of an Eastern European bag lady.

In another part of the same cemetery, those with more literary knowledge—a group of university arts students—got a glimpse into the eyes of Oscar Wilde. From all accounts the looks of surprise were reciprocated.

These revelations were only momentary, but enough to send chills up the students' spines. Some teachers, not having seen the stripped down shades, were dubious about their claims. Other more open-minded teachers, however, reading the reactions as genuine, encouraged their students to make contact. The shades were as non-responsive as shades normally were. This left doubts in the young minds, but the damage was not permanent.

Later, beneath the same city, tourists walking the dark subterranean corridors of the catacombs were presented with the unsettling sight of thousands of human bones reconfiguring themselves. Unlike what Anaïs had seen, the bodies did not completely reassemble themselves. In the ossuary, the rows of stacked bones and skulls found new and inventive ways to depict shapes other than the usual patterns of crosses.

As visitors were only permitted to travel single file, and the lighting was dim, many questioned what they had seen. Were they merely tricks of the eyes? Nevertheless, they made a swift exit. The place was eerie enough without sensing something not altogether natural moving around in the darkness.

Not all visitors were so fortunate.

One woman required resuscitation after passing out. Alone at the time, her shrill screams, which were swiftly cut off, alerted the ossuary's caretakers to her predicament. For them it was all in a day's work. They paid little attention to the claims of what she had seen—that the skulls had formed themselves into a giant face and then blinked at her. In their experience, even under normal circumstances, the most strong-willed came out of the morbid corridors white-faced.

The World Witch Organisation received wind of these occurrences. Although they did not see them first-hand, it was much cause for concern. Still fighting to control the eruption at Mount Etna, Caput Mortuum assigned Sojourner Pink to the task of convening the Organisation.

Once assembled, a short time later, the discussions among the Organisation's members were heated. Particularly as to why the shades were now appearing at the place of their burial. This was unusual behaviour. Shades were not only disguised, but almost always transported to another far-flung part of the globe. Usually a great distance from the site of their demise.

Unfortunately, no one knew how this means of shade control had originally been put in place. Almost seven hundred years had passed since its inception in the aftermath of the Black Death. The oldest of the current witches were far younger.

Coupled with the fact that no contemporary witches had first-hand knowledge of the shade control, and that it had not been passed down—possibly to prevent anyone meddling with the magic incorporated—the Organisation was at a loss concerning what to do with the situation. None had the skills to counter the current effects of shade revelation.

Although not an ideal ploy, it was decided that a strategy of watch and wait was all they could do. The witches dispersed and set about distributing themselves over the surface of the planet.

The observation, and the wait, began.

CATAMARINE

The room they stepped into had the dimensions and rounded shape of the hold of an enormous upturned ship. Massive arched oak beams traversed the room like ribs. They supported sizeable steel plates which were bolted one over another. They completely covered the walls and ceiling. The floor was no floor all, but a large pond surrounded on all sides by wooden decking. Floating in the centre of the pond, the smooth hull of a most extraordinary vessel glistened in the floodlights.

Anaïs was awestruck. 'That looks more like a rocket than a boat.'

'Yeah,' said Ella. 'It puts the speedboat on Sicily to shame, doesn't it?'

'It certainly does. I dare not ask if it works.'

Ella flashed her eyes. Sarcastically, she feigned insult. 'When has anything not worked, Anaïs?'

The little witch cracked a smile. 'In that case, I'm afraid to ask if you know how to drive it.'

'Anaïs, I'm a certified petrol-head.' Ella set her fists on her hips. 'I can, and will, drive anything that goes like a bat out of hell.'

'I always found that a strange expression.'

Ella frowned. 'What?'

'Bat out of hell,' replied Anaïs. 'Even if there is a hell, why would a bat in its right mind be there? With all that fire it must be bright. Bats like the dark. And it would be fried to a crisp in an instant.'

'Point taken. Can't disagree with that logic,' said Ella with a grin. She ran her eyes over the vessel's sleek lines. 'Anyway, I'm sure this goes a lot faster than a bat.'

Anaïs joined her in assessing the ship. 'How did you find it?'

'Let's just say I'm extremely inquisitive and love a challenge. I went exploring and found this door.' She flicked her thumb at the entrance behind them.

The circular door which served as the entrance was about a metre thick. More than anything, it resembled the particularly large door of a bank vault.

'The fact it was locked made me even more curious,' said Ella.

Anaïs scrutinised the door. Ringing its circumference and set into the door's edge were a series of sizeable metal bolts. 'Even to my untrained eye that's one serious-looking locking mechanism.'

Who are they trying to keep out? mused the witch. She swept the thought aside. 'How did you get in, Ella?'

The Apothecary reached into her coat. She pulled out a set of skeleton keys and jangled them in front of the witch's nose. 'Apothecary magic. There's not a door

I've found which cannot be opened.' She cocked her head at the entrance. 'Although, this one was a pretty hard nut to crack.'

Anaïs nodded at the boat. 'So, what is it?'

Ella walked along the decking to the boat's stern. Anaïs followed. Rounding the rear of the vessel she was surprised to see it had twin hulls.

'I think it's some sort of cross between a submarine and a catamaran,' said Ella, indicating the hulls. 'We are several metres below sea level, so I can only assume we have to travel underwater to get out of here. I thought we could call it "The Catamarine".' Ella tilted her head to the ceiling. She eyed the steel sheeting. Dirty brown traces of rust surrounded the joints between the sheets. The Apothecary scratched her chin. 'Unless the ceiling opens and it flies, of course, which I suppose is also a distinct possibility. I've kind of come to expect the unexpected.'

'I doubt it would fly.' Anaïs rubbed her chin. 'Something like this screaming across the sky would definitely draw attention to itself. Not to mention screaming across water. You might be right with the submarine idea. Keeping a low profile is the first rule of witchdom.'

'Does that include volcanic eruptions?'

Anaïs paled. 'Um … yes, I suppose so.'

'Sorry.' Ella placed a comforting hand on Anaïs's shoulder. 'I shouldn't have said that.'

'It's okay,' said Anaïs reservedly. 'Even though it's terrible what happened, from the point of view of the rest of the world I expect the eruption would be seen as a natural disaster.'

Ella nodded in agreement.

'But that thing'—Anaïs waved her hand at the Catamarine—'is far from natural.'

She walked along the decking towards the prow, admiring its streamlined form. About five metres wide and ten metres long, it resembled twin rockets. The rounded sterns tapered into sharp points at the bow. Connecting the hulls and protruding atop the bow was what appeared to be a cabin, presumably the wheelhouse. The entire vessel was covered in gleaming aluminium sheeting which emphasised its rocket-like appearance.

Anaïs took a deep breath and expelled it loudly. 'Okay!'

'Okay?'

'Okay, let's go. We have a destination.' Anaïs flipped her thumb at the vessel. 'And now transportation.'

'That we do!' exclaimed a delighted Ella. Her voice rang loudly around the cavernous space, bouncing off the steel walls. She cupped her mouth with a hand. Dropping it, she said, 'Sorry, it's kind of exciting.'

Anaïs grinned. 'Yes, it is. Thank goodness for your enthusiasm, Ella. I don't know how I would get by without it.' She paused. 'Only, how do we get on board?'

Ella pointed above them at a gangplank secured to the wall. A ladder ran up the wall to give access to it. 'My guess is you swing that thing out and climb on it?'

Anaïs grinned. 'The solutions never stop with you, do they?'

Ella laughed. 'Nope.'

A tremor sent vibrations through the boards beneath their feet and a ripple across the pond.

'We better hurry,' said Ella, watching the ripples causing small waves to lap against the hull of the Catamarine. 'You get the others and I'll check this thing out.'

'Right you are,' said Anaïs as she made her way to the door. 'Don't leave without me.'

'Ha!' Ella smirked. 'I wouldn't dream of it, Anaïs.'

SUBMERGED

Nonplussed, Anaïs stared at the collection of instruments set into the console before her. She glanced at Ella. 'You were saying something about a petrol-head being able to drive this?'

Ella shrugged. 'I'm sure I'll be fine once I find the accelerator pedal.'

'I think you will need to know more than that to get this thing going.'

Ella smiled. 'I'm well aware of that. It was a joke. Boats don't have accelerator pedals anyway. There must be some way to start it though.' She frowned, studying the console. 'Let's try this.' She twirled her finger in the air and jammed it down on a large green button in the centre of the console.

Deep within the bowels of the vessel they heard a ticking followed by the syncopated thump of an engine winding itself up. A tremor similar to the one they had experienced on the boardwalk sent vibrations through the soles of their shoes.

'Well,' said Ella. 'That answers that mystery.'

'Okay, but how do we get rid of that.' Anaïs indicated the gangplank connecting the wheelhouse to the wall of the cavern.

'With this.' Ella produced a small, elongated yellow box. On top of it were several buttons and two levers. Ella walked across the wheelhouse. Leaning out the door in order to see what she was doing, she pressed one of the buttons. Using the levers, she guided the gangplank away from the Catamarine until it was flush with the wall. She secured the door. Moving back across the wheelhouse, she dropped the controller on the console.

Anaïs eyed the little box. 'How many of those things do you actually have?'

'A few,' said Ella. 'Generally one of them will operate any equipment I come across.'

'Did you have a look downstairs?' enquired Anaïs, indicating the circular stairwell positioned in the far corner of the wheelhouse.

'No.' Ella shook her head. 'No time. I think it's better if we get going first. Will the others be all right?'

'I'm sure they'll be fine down there with Immi,' said Anaïs. She grinned. 'Although, I doubt Immi is fine with them. But hey, she can make herself useful. We have enough to do here without her interfering.'

'Right you are. Let's get moving.' Ella ran her fingers over the buttons on the console. She pressed one with a large downward facing arrow on it.

Anaïs glanced out the window. A row of louvres set low in the wall and running around the circumference of the room opened. Water began gushing in. It streamed over the wooden decking.

'The door!' yelled Anaïs, gesticulating at the entrance to the dock.

Ella glanced around the console in panic. 'I don't see anything that looks like a door. Do you?'

Anaïs joined her in frantically searching for a button which might correspond with the door to the subterranean boathouse. 'No, nothing. Can't we just push something? Anything?'

'Nope.'

'What do you mean "nope"?'

Considering their predicament, Ella's voice seemed unusually calm. 'Look.' She indicated the door. As the water washed towards it, the enormous vault door began to close. 'It's automatic.' She patted her chest to sooth her pounding heart. 'Had me going there for a bit. At least now we know why this place has such a door.'

Anaïs nodded. She watched the water's progress. 'I'm confused. How did you know what to press? It can't be pot luck.'

'Most of it's pretty obvious and straightforward.' Ella pointed at the button she had pushed. 'It's a down arrow, right? However, I have to admit I did peruse the manual while I was waiting for you.' She flicked her head towards the thick book lying on one of the two helmsman's chairs.

Anaïs's eyes widened. 'That's a lot of book to peruse.'

'I'm a speed-reader. Also, I read a lot. I can't tell you

how many manuals I've read. They're all pretty much the same once you get the hang of them.'

'I hate manuals.'

Ella smiled. 'Well then, it's a good thing you have me around.'

'Indeed it is.' The witch's eyes widened. 'Whoa!'

Water began lapping over the top of the hull and splashing onto the wheelhouse's windows.

'I hope this is safe.'

'It's a bit late to consider that now,' said Ella. She stared intently at the dials on the console.

Anaïs eyed the windows of the wheelhouse. Apprehensively, she watched the water level rise until they were fully submerged. Seeing that there were no leakages she relaxed a little.

As it rose, the water in the pond began churning. It continued rising steadily until, apart from the odd air bubble playing over the steel plating above them, the boathouse was completely filled.

The Catamarine shuddered and began to sink. Through the murky water Anaïs watched the curved ceiling of the room recede as they slowly descended. Without warning, the floodlighting in the boathouse doused itself, plunging them into darkness.

The lighting in the wheelhouse brightened, adjusting automatically to the gloom. Anaïs peered through the window but could barely see the bow of the vessel.

'I can't see a thing,' said Anaïs. 'And you?'

Ella looked up from the console. She shook her head. 'No. Hang on a second.' She reached over to the far side of the console and flicked a switch. Instantly several floodlights on the gunwale of the vessel lit up their surroundings.

'Wow!' exclaimed Anaïs.

The strong lights penetrated deep into the darkness, illuminating the murky water for several metres in all directions.

'It's like a forest,' said Anaïs, marvelling at the plethora of pylons around them.

'The whole city is build on wooden poles. Pretty cool, eh?'

'Yes, but how will we get out of here without bringing the city down around us? This thing is pretty big.'

Ella picked up the vessel's manual and flipped through the pages. 'Here! The boat has an autopilot. We just need to give it a destination.'

'Well, we have that.' She pulled out her promptuary. 'Show me what you did before,' she commanded it.

The handbook obliged, displaying the holographic map of lost souls. She pointed at the island Ella had indicated earlier. 'What are the coordinates of this place?' The map vanished, replaced by a digital counter on the open pages. The promptuary scrolled through numbers before stopping.

'Can you read that, Ella?'

'Yes.' Ella closed the manual and dropped it on the floor at her feet. She typed the cyphers into a keypad on the console. She glanced at Anaïs. 'Are we ready?'

Anaïs smiled. 'We better be.'

'Hold on. It might be a good idea to sit down. I have no idea how fast this thing goes.'

Anaïs shut her handbook. She set the promptuary down on the console and settled into one of the chairs. Both seats were bolted to the floor. She rocked in it to test its rigidity and gripped the armrests in anticipation. Ella leaned over the console. Her finger hovered over the green button. 'Are you sure?'

'No, Ella, I'm never sure. But what other option do we have?' Anaïs took a deep breath. Exhaling, she tightened her grip on the armrests. 'Do it!'

The Apothecary pressed the button. She slid into the other seat and gripped her own armrests.

Nothing happened.

Anaïs and Ella glanced at one another.

'Ahem …' said the Apothecary.

Suddenly, a loud horn began whooping, followed by a deep rumbling within the vessel. The horn ceased, its sound replaced with the thundering throb of the vessel's power source. Ever so slowly, the Catamarine inched forward. Soft music began piping from speakers embedded in the ceiling of the wheelhouse.

Ella screwed up her face. 'Huh? The Beach Boys?'

'Who are they?'

'You don't know?' Ella furrowed her brow and snorted. 'Weird. But this isn't so …'

Her sentence was interrupted. The vessel shot forward, flinging her to the back of her seat.

'What the—!'

The two women shot fearful sideways glances at one another before fixing their eyes on the path ahead. The Catamarine threaded its way at breakneck speed between the pylons. It barely had room to fit through some of the narrowest spaces. Occasionally, it scraped one of the underwater tree trunks, causing the hull to ring like a bell.

Anaïs closed her eyes and dug her fingers into the armrests. She caught her breath and forced herself to regulate it. *Keep calm. All will be fine. Trust it.*

INTO THE ADRIATIC

Following the initial spurt of the vessel accelerating, it settled into cruising speed. The loud thumping noise of the motor subsided to a droning hum. It continued to wend its way skilfully through the underwater forest supporting the city. Gradually the forest thinned and the pylons disappeared altogether, leaving them in open water.

Ella prodded the witch. 'It's okay, Anaïs. You can look.'

Anaïs opened her eyes and stared through the windscreen. The floodlights now barely permeated the muddy waters. They were sailing blind. Satisfied that it was safe to get up, Anaïs slid off her seat. She smirked at the Apothecary. 'Did that meet your petrol-head expectations?'

The Apothecary smiled and nodded vigorously. 'Yes, it did. Whoever built this thing and the tube must have been like-minded souls. Although, I would have preferred a warning.'

'There was a warning. The horn.'

'Yeah,' said Ella. 'But that could have meant anything. Abandon ship, for instance.'

'Let's hope we don't have to contend with something like that,' said Anaïs. 'We managed to get out of the city, so I'm sure we'll be fine.'

'I hope so.'

Anaïs retrieved her promptuary and commanded it to display a map of their location and surroundings. She scrutinised it closely, watching their progress. They had left the confines of the city and now cruised across the lagoon. Within a short period of time, they skirted the island of Lido, exited the lagoon and moved out into the open waters of the Adriatic. 'We're really moving. We'll be there in no time.'

Ella checked their speed and position on a dial on the console. She did a quick mental calculation. 'I think we have about an hour or two. That is, if we don't hit any obstacles.'

'Great!' said Anaïs cheerfully. 'Then I'm going to have a look around.'

'I better stay here. Can you leave your promptuary?'

'I'm not sure if that's possible,' said Anaïs. 'It usually attaches itself to me. But we can give it a try.'

'Maybe we can try this.' At one end of the console was a pair of fasteners. The Apothecary slipped the edges of the book's cover under them. She secured the fasteners with the thumbscrews attached to them. 'Looks like they were made for this.'

'Yes it does,' agreed Anaïs.

'Try to go for a walk across the room.'

Anaïs walked across to the stairwell. She heard the screws creak in protest as the promptuary strained on its bindings. Its pages flapped, but the map floating above them remained intact.

'It seems to work,' said Anaïs. 'Probably best I don't stay away too long. It looks pretty secure, but we wouldn't want it flying through the ship, would we?'

'No,' said Ella shaking her head. 'I don't think that would be a good idea.'

'See you soon.'

'Are you sure?'

Anaïs nodded, then hesitated. She eyed her promptuary dubiously before deciding it was safe to leave. She began to descend the circular stairwell. She had not been separated from it since Amalfi. An odd feeling overcame her. As if she was leaving part of herself behind. An unseen force wrenched at her, almost as if her skin were being pulled from her bones. She averted her eyes from the handbook and sent out her thoughts to it. '*Don't worry, I'll be back.*' Curiously the pull waned.

She continued down the stairs. Reaching the bottom she stepped off the last tread onto a polished marble floor. Mouth agape, her eyes widened in amazement. A room of incredible proportions greeted her. It reminded her of the internals of the train she had caught from England to France. Not only due to the generous size of the space but also how luxuriously it was appointed. However, whereas the furnishings in the train had been antique, the fittings here were much more contemporary. It reminded her of the Art Deco sets of Hollywood movies from the 1930s.

Polished walnut appeared to be the predominant choice of wood. The walls were lined with it. The sleek furniture, which was secured to the walls, was also constructed from walnut. The room was oval. Semi-circular couches jutted out from the walls. Set into the ceiling, about three metres above her head, was a large round light fitting. In its centre was a skylight. Reminiscent of the one in the train, it displayed the sky above. The arrowed formation of a flock of geese flew overhead. She watched their structured flight pattern. *Some things in nature are so magical.* Her view of the birds was momentarily blocked as they passed beneath the hull of an enormous ocean liner. *That thing definitely needs a clean.*

She dropped her gaze and assessed the rest of the room. Set into the walls at the far end were bookshelves. She walked over to one set of shelves. The books on them were ancient. She selected one and pulled it off the shelf. There were no words on its spine, only the stylised symbol of a human form. She flipped through the pages. They were thick and coarse to the touch, not thin and smooth like modern paper. Her eyes roved over the pages. She stopped flipping and studied a page. There were no words, only symbols. She scratched her head. *Hieroglyphics?*

Anaïs gently stroked the page with her fingertips. She felt the bumps of the symbols as her fingers ran over them. She marvelled at the age of the object she held in her hand. She considered her own predicament. *Will I ever get this old?*

She closed the book and set it back on the shelf, sliding it into the space it had vacated. She ran her thumb over the spine. She smiled. *I hope not. Nobody wants to be shelved.*

She turned and scanned the room. *Where are the others?*

'Immi? Nan?' she called out.

Hearing no response, she raised her voice and yelled their names again. Still nothing. She searched for a door. Finding one behind the stairwell, she opened it. On the other side was a dimly lit corridor.

She yelled down the corridor, 'Immi! Nan!'

From a distance came a reply. 'Anaïs? Is that you?' Although barely audible, the voice was clearly the librarian's.

'Yes,' shouted Anaïs. 'Where are you?'

'Here.'

Anaïs frowned. 'That doesn't help. Can you come to me?'

'No. I'm lost. I don't know where you are.'

Anaïs sighed. 'Sheesh!' She stared down the long corridor. It was lined with doors on both sides. *How big is this thing?* She projected her voice. 'Hang on! I'm coming! Keep calling my name! I'll find you!'

Immi did as instructed. Homing in on the librarian's voice, Anaïs set off down the corridor.

DOWN BELOW

Still calling the librarian's name, Anaïs continued until she reached the end of the corridor. She opened the door before her. Finding herself in a small anteroom, she was confronted with more doors. She slapped her forehead. *How many rooms does this thing have?*

She called out to the librarian. Immi replied. Her voice was less distant than it had been. Anaïs chose the door through which the sound came. Beyond it was another corridor. *Whew! This place is a maze. I better keep track of where I've been.*

She rummaged in her beret and found what she was looking for: a piece of chalk. She scrawled a purple cross on the door leading to the first corridor. She admired her handiwork and grinned. *I'm never going to tire of that colour.*

Moving to the end of the corridor, she passed through another door into another anteroom. It too was lined with doors. *Man! Does this ever end?* She scrawled a cross on the door to the corridor and yelled out to Immi. The shrill voice of the librarian came through a door to her right. *Really close now.*

Opening the door, she stepped into a large room. The entire space was pristine white. The walls were lined with familiar-looking drawers. A pin-point of light burned in the centre of the face of each drawer. *Wow! A mobile apotheek. Ella will be pleased.*

'Thank goodness!' exclaimed Immi from across the room. 'Whatever you do, don't let the door shut.'

Anaïs frowned. 'Why?'

'It disappears.'

Holding the door ajar, Anaïs poked her head around it. The internal face was handleless and coated in the same immaculate white as the rest of the room. 'Oh! I see.'

'You didn't think we were that stupid, did you?'

'Well—'

'Wrong question,' said Immi, rolling her eyes. 'Forget I asked it. Please keep your thoughts to yourself.'

'Okay.'

'What's going on up there?' enquired the librarian, pointing at the ceiling.

'We're moving.'

'I gathered that. And fast. There's nothing to hang onto in here, you know. This thing is dangerous.' Immi massaged her shoulder. She glanced around the white room. 'It felt like being in a padded cell without the padding.'

Anaïs looked at the shades. *'Are you guys okay?'*

'Yes,' they all chimed simultaneously.

'Good.' She smiled at them. The old woman who was Nan, the bodybuilder and the ghost-like child stood in a tight group across the room. *What a collection I have here.* Anaïs turned her attention back to the librarian. 'Have you checked out the rest of the boat? Or is this as far as you got?'

'Pretty much,' said Immi. 'This thing is huge. We explored a bit, found this room and, like I explained, the door shut behind us. Then we were stuck. The boat, or whatever it is, took off and we were thrown around the room. Scary as hell when you don't know what's happening.'

'It's not actually a boat. More a kind of submarine. And we didn't know what it would do either.

'A submarine! So now we're underwater?'

Anaïs nodded. 'Yep.'

'Glad I didn't know that before,' said Immi, shaking her head. She twisted her lips and murmured, 'Probably better I couldn't see what was going on.'

'Probably,' agreed Anaïs.

'Where are we now?'

'We're sailing beneath the Adriatic and heading to Greece.'

'Why Greece?'

'Long story,' said the little witch. 'Just trying to get us safe.'

'Safe from what?'

'There's a lot of activity going on up there.' She nodded her head at the white slate of the ceiling above her.

'Activity?' enquired Immi with concern.

'Weird stuff.'

'Stuff?'

'Better you don't know.'

Immi glanced warily at the ceiling. She dropped her eyes, examining the witch's face. 'I'd rather know what I'm in for, Anaïs. You said nothing at the house. Only that we had to get out fast.'

'Immi, you really don't want to know,' said Anaïs, dropping her own eyes to avoid the librarian's worried stare. 'I'm not so sure what's going on myself. When I find out you'll be the first to hear.'

The librarian frowned. 'Somehow I don't believe you.'

'Just trust me, Immi.'

'Trust?'

'Yes.'

Immi's knee-jerk response was to protest. With some effort she stopped herself. She pondered the witch's answer for a moment. 'Okay,' she relented. 'I suppose I don't have a choice.'

'No, not really.'

'Great!' The librarian rolled her eyes again. It took every ounce of her willpower to suppress the urge to berate the witch. She breathed deeply to calm herself. 'Can you at least tell me what's in Greece?'

'It's the nearest place where I'm reasonably sure we won't be bothered,' said Anaïs. 'Then I will have a chance to think and work out what to do next.'

'Oh good,' said Immi. 'So you have a plan?'

Anaïs shook her head. 'Not exactly.'

Immi eyed her dubiously. 'So are we just running away then?'

She hunched her shoulders. 'To begin with, yes, I suppose. But it's a start.'

'Doesn't sound like much of a plan.'

'A half-baked plan is better than no plan at all.'

Immi opened her mouth to respond but was interrupted. Above her a speaker recessed into the ceiling crackled loudly. Anaïs heard the unsettling sound of panic in the Apothecary's voice. 'Anaïs … Anaïs? Can you hear me? We have a problem. You better get up here. Now!'

THE CANAL

In the wheelhouse Ella was beside herself. 'I think we're stuck.'

'Stuck?'

'Look.' Ella indicated the three-dimensional map displayed by the promptuary.

Anaïs peered at it. She removed the handbook from its fasteners. Holding it flat on one palm, she pivoted it around with her other hand to get a better look at their surroundings. 'I don't see the problem. It's just a canal.'

'Yes,' said Ella. 'The Corinth Canal. But it's not very wide or deep.'

Anaïs shrugged. 'It looks wide enough to me. I'm sure we'll fit.'

'I think it's risky.'

'You think too much.'

'I could say the same about you.' Ella smiled. 'Like I said, it's not very deep, Anaïs. We might have to surface. That's not a good idea. People will spot us.'

Anaïs frowned. 'Mmm … we wouldn't want that. If

you're worried about it, Ella, we can go back and find another way.'

'Maybe that's better.'

Setting it back down on the console, Anaïs instructed the promptuary to zoom out and find another route. It displayed an alternative. 'That's a long way. We would have to backtrack and then go all the way around the bottom of Greece.'

'Greece has quite a big bottom,' observed the Apothecary.

Anaïs began to giggle.

'What? Uh—oh!' Ella began to laugh as well. She smothered her mouth with her hand. Clearing her throat, she regained her composure. 'Big bottom or not, we don't have much choice. Better to deal with a long trip rather than risk revealing ourselves. Are we in that much of a hurry anyway?' She scrutinised the map. 'It's not as far as we've come already. It wouldn't take long. This thing moves fast.'

'Hey, guys.'

Anaïs sighed. She glanced over her shoulder. 'Yes, Immi?'

The librarian had followed her up from the hold. In her haste to find out about Ella's problem, Anaïs had forgotten she was present. The fact she had been silent for so long was also out of character.

'We have another problem,' said Immi. 'Going back may not be possible.'

Irritated, Anaïs knotted her brow. 'What do you mean?'

'Look there.' The librarian pointed at a number of dots on the map to the rear of the Catamarine.

Ella watched the pinpoints gathering together. She rubbed her chin. 'What is that?'

'Beats me,' said Anaïs. 'Doesn't this thing have a periscope or something?'

'Haven't found one,' said Ella. 'We would have to surface to find out what it is. What about your promptuary? Can't it help?'

'What's this?' said Immi. Before Ella and Anaïs could stop her, she punched a large button embedded in the rear wall of the wheelhouse. They were plunged into darkness.

'Immi!' cried Anaïs. 'You idiot! What have you done?'

'Don't call me an idiot!'

Slowly, light began to return. Firstly, a kind of grey-blue twilight. Then rays of filtered light began to appear. The entire vessel had dematerialised. They were surrounded on all sides by water. Anaïs felt as though she were floating—but then again, not. She could still sense the solidity of the deck beneath her feet. It was disconcerting. Awestruck, she watched the rays of light playing in the sea water.

'What's going on?' cried the librarian. 'Are we drowning?'

Anaïs snorted. 'Can you breathe?'

'Yes.' The librarian inhaled deeply to make certain.

'Then you're not drowning.'

'Oh. Okay,' said Immi reservedly.

'We're still in the ship,' said Ella. 'Only, it's become invisible.'

'Very cool!' exclaimed Anaïs. 'Immi, don't you dare touch anything else.'

'There's nothing *to* touch!' Red-faced and flustered, the librarian took a few short breaths in an attempt to calm herself. She cleared her throat. 'At least now we know what that button does.'

'You have a point, but I think we better let Ella take care of stuff like this in future.'

The librarian shrugged. 'Whatever you say.'

Gradually, more details of their surroundings materialised. Beneath them, long strands of sea grass swayed in the current. A school of fish flew over the witch's head. She ducked instinctively. Embarrassed by her reaction, she glanced at the others. Immi and Ella were both in a crouching position. Gingerly, they all stood up.

'This is going to take a bit of getting used to,' said Ella.

The librarian and Anaïs both nodded in agreement.

The light around them increased, allowing more detail to appear. To the rear the hulls of a number of large ships materialised. They were clearly queuing up to enter the canal. All were approaching at a rapid rate. The lead vessel was towed by a tug boat. As it neared them, the water it churned up obscured the rest of the vessels.

'We can't get past them,' observed Ella. 'It's too shallow.'

'Then we have no alternative,' said Anaïs. 'We have to go through the canal. And quickly. Let's get moving.'

'With what?' said Ella, sweeping her arm around her. 'Where's the control console?'

'It must be here,' said Anaïs, glancing around her and trying to subdue the panic rising inside her. 'We can't see it, that's all.'

'Not handy,' said Ella. 'This is a cool idea, but not very practical.'

'Immi,' said Anaïs. 'Feel around. Find the button.'

'Everything's invisible. I can't see a thing.'

'None of us can. But it must be there somewhere. You were right next to it.'

The librarian began slapping the air around her. Watching her, Anaïs had a passing thought that, had the situation not been so serious, her movements would have been hilarious.

'Ow!' cried Immi. She shook her wrist and massage her hand. 'That's the wall.'

Anaïs eyed the ship bearing down on them. She danced on the spot. 'Don't stop. Just keep hitting it.'

Immi did as she was told. Gingerly, she patted the invisible wall. Suddenly, the unrestricted view of their surroundings flickered. Then it disappeared altogether, plunging them into complete darkness. Hysteria set in. Both Anaïs and Ella hurled abuse at Immi.

To everyone's relief the blackout was momentary. The previous unrestricted view of their surroundings began to rematerialise.

'Aargh!' shouted Anaïs. 'It didn't work!'

The librarian's face turned white. She panicked and

frantically began slapping the invisible wall with both hands.

'Stop!' yelled Anaïs. 'Look!'

Although not completely solid, the outline of the wheelhouse and its internal structure began to reappear. The semi-transparent console took on a glass-like form. The instruments on it regenerated. In the centre, the shape of a large button appeared.

'There!' cried Anaïs. 'Punch it, Ella!'

The Apothecary jammed her thumb down on the button. The low thud of the Catamarine's idling power source increased in volume. Anaïs spun on the spot. The tugboat was almost upon them. Water churned around them, obscuring the view to the rear of the Catamarine. It was not generated by the tugboat. Their own vessel's wake created the disturbance. They began to move forward. At first, the movement was barely perceptible. Within moments the vessel began to build up speed.

The banks of the bay they were in swiftly closed in around them. The waterway narrowed until the entrance to the canal loomed before them. With it, the water became shallower, forcing the Catamarine to rise until they were just beneath the surface. Towering above them, the steep, vertical, manmade sides of the canal came into view.

The Catamarine continued to accelerate. Anaïs watched water to the sides of the vessel, and behind it, displace. Ploughing through the shallows, the waves it caused washed up the cliff faces.

Anaïs had a momentary mental flashback of their journey through the tunnels below Sicily in the

Dreadnought. That had been freaky enough. This was worse. At least then she could see the vessel she was travelling in. Seemingly standing in nothingness, with water swirling around her—yet not touching her—it was as if she moved in an impenetrable giant air bubble. The sensation was incredibly disconcerting.

She watched the wash of the Catamarine thrown up behind them. Thoughts raced through her head. *This canal better be short or we'll be noticed. Maybe we'll be mistaken for a fish. Do they have whales in the Mediterranean?*

The answer came quickly. Within minutes they had exited the tunnel-like confines of the canal into open water. Anaïs, Ella and Immi glanced at one another. Collectively, they expelled a deep sigh of relief.

THE ISLAND

The map the promptuary displayed indicated that they had arrived at their destination: the Greek island of Delos.

'We'll have to stop here,' said Ella. 'I can't get us any closer or we'll run aground.'

Anaïs scrutinised the promptuary. They were still quite some way offshore. 'How will we get ashore?'

'Maybe we should search the Catamarine.' Ella ran her eyes around the wheelhouse. 'There must be a lifeboat or something.'

Anaïs shook her head. 'I didn't see one.'

'Let's just surface and take it from there.'

'Okay.'

To the relief of all, during the journey and after consulting the vessel's manual, Ella had managed to find the correct sequence of buttons enabling the Catamarine to resume its solid form. The Apothecary adjusted the dials on the console. She twirled her finger in the air and punched a button with an arrow pointing upwards. From deep within the bowels of the vessel, Anaïs heard loud rushing, the sound strangely akin to the noise from a washing machine on spin cycle. Through the thick glass of the cabin she watched the water churn. Thousands of bubbles swept past the window and made their way to the surface. After a short pause the Catamarine began to rise with them. Within moments they had surfaced.

As the last rivulets of water ran down the windows, the view outside cleared. Their surroundings came into focus. The sight of a cloudless blue sky caused Anaïs to sigh. She realised that during her time underwater an uncomfortable feeling of confinement had seeped in. *It's gonna be so good to breathe fresh air again.*

She walked across the cabin and opened the hatch. The rubber seals squeaked loudly as she swung it open. She gripped the door frame, leaned forward, and stuck her head outside. She smiled as a light breeze caressed her cheeks. She took a deep breath, drawing the salty air into her lungs. She expelled it. 'Ah!'

Anaïs stepped out onto the bulkhead. Only the wheelhouse and a raised platform around it had surfaced. It was slippery, and she had to make certain of her footing before stepping away from the door. She eyed the island. Judging the distance, she ascertained that she could swim it if need be.

'I'll go see if I can find a lifeboat.'

Ella's voice snapped Anaïs out of her thoughts. It took her by surprise and made her jump. She lost her footing. Skating on the wet surface, she practically did the splits before regaining her balance.

The Apothecary had to stifle laughter at the sight. She quickly apologised. 'Sorry, I didn't mean to startle you.'

Her face flushed red with embarrassment, Anaïs cleared her throat. 'No problem.' She searched the hull for a handgrip. She found one in the form of the sill of the wheelhouse window. 'Yes, good idea, Ella. I'll wait here while you look.'

Ella smiled. 'Good. I'll be right back. You be careful, all right?'

Anaïs nodded.

The Apothecary walked across to the stairwell and descended. Immi took her place and stuck her head out the door.

'It looks deserted,' she said. 'What the hell are we doing here anyway?'

'The promptuary suggested it.'

'So, we're just going to wait around here?'

'I suppose so,' said Anaïs. 'Do you have any other ideas?'

Immi shrugged. 'Nope.'

'Then you answered your own question.'

A noise caught Anaïs's ear. She glanced down at the water lapping against the hull. It began to bubble and churn. Anaïs looked towards the island. The churning was not only next to the Catamarine but carved a thick line between it and the land. Anaïs stared at the peculiarity. She scratched her head. *What the heck is happening now?*

Slightly fearful, with her back to it, Anaïs shimmied along the window to get closer to the door. The churning grew louder. She watched with curiosity as, from beneath the agitated water, a solid form began to surface. The foaming water subsided. A stone walkway appeared, connecting the vessel to the island.

'Ahem …' said Anaïs, nonplussed.

'I think that solves the land-access problem,' said Immi.

Anaïs rolled her eyes. 'I can see that! Why do you always have to state the bleeding obvious?'

'I don't,' protested the librarian.

'You—' Anaïs stopped herself, realising expressing her irritation with the librarian would be counter-productive. She exhaled. 'Sorry, Immi. I'm a little on edge. I honestly don't know what to do next.'

'I totally get that,' said Immi, adopting a reassuring tone. 'Apology accepted. Perhaps you should just go with your intuition.'

'You're right. It's worked so far.' Anaïs examined the walkway. 'I guess I'll be going for a stroll then.'

'Are you sure it's safe?'

'No,' said Anaïs. 'But, for whatever reason, it's here now. We should make use of it.'

'We? Shouldn't we wait for Ella?'

'No. I don't think so. It might disappear.' Anaïs calculated how long it would take her to run across the walkway. 'I'm going!'

'What?'

Anaïs stepped forward and climbed over the railing encircling the platform.

'No, wait!' cried Immi.

Anaïs ignored her. She knotted her brow and

focussed, setting her sights on the other end of the walkway. She bent her knees and prepared to sprint.

Pushing herself off the railing she leapt over the small gap between the platform and the walkway. Partially covered in a layer of algae, the stonework's surface was slimy. Anaïs almost lost her balance. Managing to stay upright, she continued. She pumped her legs and ran for all she was worth. Like a speed-skater, slipping and sliding with each step, she made it across the narrow causeway.

Close to shore she locked her knees and glided sideways across the damp stonework. At the last minute she crouched and launched herself over the gap at the end. To her relief she landed safely with both feet firmly planted in the soft mud on the shoreline.

Panting, she grinned at her good fortune.

Extracting her boots one at a time, she stepped up onto the dried-out mud shales before her. She turned to face the boat. Standing in the Catamarine's doorway, Immi was yelling and gesticulating wildly. Anaïs heard nothing, the librarian's voice lost in the sea breeze. She glanced down at the water. It was churning and foaming again. With a loud gurgle the stone walkway sank below the surface.

Anaïs's shoulders slumped. *Oh no!*

DELOS

The little witch watched helplessly as, on the deck of the Catamarine, Immi and Ella discussed the new situation. It was clear to Anaïs that Ella had been unsuccessful in her search for a lifeboat.

She sat down on a large rock. Staring at her muddy boots, she contemplated what to do. She was stranded.

She sighed. 'Now what am I going to do?'

A commotion on the boat caused her to raise her head. She frowned. An object shot out through the wheelhouse's open doorway. It zipped across the strip of water towards her.

What is that?

She had no time to scoot around the rock. She cowered. Raising her hands palms-out she formed a barrier before her face. The object hit her palms and stuck. The impact almost toppled her backwards over the rock. She lowered her hands and looked at the object in them. She smiled. The promptuary had returned to its mistress.

She ran her finger over the star on its cover and hugged the book to her chest. 'Hello, old friend.'

A calmness came over her. Having the handbook back in her possession gave her the confidence to go on. She removed her beret and dropped the promptuary into it. Silently commanding the book to stay put, she set the beret back on her head.

'Right! Let's do some exploring.'

She stood and waved to the boat's occupants. She pointed behind her indicating that she would go inland. They gestured emphatically that they disagreed. Anaïs shook her head vigorously. She gave them a thumbs-up and yelled, 'I'll be all right!'

Their body language clearly indicated that they found it a less-than-ideal course of action.

Sorry, guys, a witch has got to do what a witch has got to do.

She turned her back on them and climbed the slope of the small hill. Stopping at the crest of the hill, she glanced down once more at the boat. She could no longer read the faces of her crew. They seemed so far away. Sitting out in the bay, with only its cabin and the platform surrounding it visible, the Catamarine looked like an ordinary yacht.

Anaïs grinned. *Witches are so clever.*

A breeze stirred. It whipped at her hair. Floating on the wind she heard the sound of a voice calling a single word. She listened intently. There it was again. It was the voice of a woman. She was calling out a name.

What? No! Slightly obscured by the wind, but nonetheless clear, the name was: Anaïs.

She turned away from the boat and faced inland. Her eyes roved over the landscape. From her viewpoint, on top of its highest hill, the island looked small. Beyond it she could see the blue backdrop of the waters of the Mediterranean. Surrounding it was a series of other small islands. Down below, at the foot of the hill, was what appeared to be a small town.

She heard the voice again. This time louder, it seemed to be coming from the settlement. With some trepidation Anaïs proceeded down the hill. The rocky surface made movement difficult. Before long, even though the temperature was low and the breeze fresh, she was coated in sweat.

She reached the outskirts of the town. It appeared uninhabited. The buildings she could see were roofless ancient ruins. Finding a path, she followed it until she was confronted with a row of statues in the form of imposing animals. Although their features had been eroded from centuries of being exposed to the elements, Anaïs could clearly see what they represented. Apprehensively, she eyed their elongated bodies and exposed rib cages. They made her skin crawl. *Hellhounds!*

'Anaïs!'

The voice was loud and urgent. More direct and no longer only carried by the wind, it cut through her ears. It echoed in her head. The source was a clump of trees. From up on the hilltop the area had caught her eye. In the barren and otherwise stony landscape, she had spotted this small oasis of green in the centre of the town.

She turned her back on the statues. Walking across the path, she passed between the trees and entered a strangely lush garden. All the while, the feeling of being watched by the stone hounds made the hair on her neck stand on end.

Ignore them! They're not real!

The garden was overgrown, and the path she followed through it narrow. The voice had stopped. It was no longer necessary. She followed her senses. They guided her to a small open area. In it a single palm tree stood, its trunk encircled by a low stone wall.

She cocked her head. 'Odd.'

From behind the tree an old woman stepped out. Her long hair was pure white except for a few strands of purple which divided it at a part in the middle of her head. Anaïs caught her breath.

With a youthful gait which did not befit her age, the woman moved towards the witch. Anaïs attempted to step away from her but found herself rooted to the spot.

'Don't be afraid, Anaïs,' said the woman. 'There's nothing to fear.'

Her voice was pure velvet. Any misgivings Anaïs had melted away. A wave of peace swept over her, such was the woman's aura.

She stepped closer to Anaïs. Reaching out she took the little witch's hands in her own. They were incredibly warm. Anaïs felt the warmth surge up her arms and flush her body. It added to the sheen of sweat which already coated her.

'I'm so glad you came, Anaïs,' said the woman quietly. 'I've been waiting for this moment for so long.' She smiled sweetly. 'It's not every day that I get to meet my only granddaughter.'

Anaïs gaped. She cleared her throat and went to speak. The woman released Anaïs's hands. She lifted a hand and pressed her index finger to the witch's lips. Just before contact a small spark of static electricity jumped between the finger and Anaïs's lips. It left them tingling.

'There's no need to speak, Anaïs,' said her grandmother. 'I have so much to tell you.' She chuckled. 'Oh my, where are my manners? Let me introduce myself properly. My name is Lilith.'

LILITH

Mythological legend has it that in the beginning it all started with a man and a woman. The man was called Adam. The woman—Lilith. Lilith and Adam were equals. They were created from the same stuff. They came out of the earth.

There was a problem. Lilith and Adam did not see eye to eye. In a sexual sense they both wanted to be on top. Adam refused to give in to Lilith's demands. She decided enough was enough and left. She did a runner.

As is the case in the breakdown of many relationships, it did not go smoothly. Adam resented the fact that Lilith had deserted him and proceeded to make all kinds of wild accusations. He spread rumours that she slept with demons and feasted on the blood of small children. He went out of his way to paint her in a negative light. Unfortunately, everyone believed him. She got a raw deal. But then, she wasn't around to defend herself. For time immemorial she became associated with evil. Some discounted the fact that she even existed.

Adam moved on. He demanded a new partner. He got Eve. Eve was certainly not Lilith. She was made from a bit of Adam. I know it's slightly a clichéd thing to say, but let's just assume Eve was a bit blonde. Apologies to all the blondes out there. No insult intended. Perhaps we should avoid the whole blonde analogy and just assume she was gullible.

Eve got Adam into all kinds of trouble. He ended up kicked out of his own house. He blamed everyone except himself. He was blinded. All he saw was Eve. Probably because Eve gave him what he wanted. She let him be on top.

This set off a pattern which was to haunt naturals for eternity: a male obsession with domination over women. If only Adam had treated Lilith exactly for what she was—an equal—then the universe would be in much better shape.

But what happened to Lilith? Nobody really knows. At least in the natural world. Mainly because everybody believed Adam. If only Lilith had employed a good lawyer and got Adam to refute his claims. Probably, she just couldn't be bothered. The guy was never going to let her be on top.

Lilith went her own way. She maintained a healthy connection with the universe, whereas Adam severed all knowledge. Much to the detriment of mankind. Adam really has a lot to answer for. From the very beginning the world went down two separate paths. One most naturals are aware of. One that has been concealed.

Lilith was the first witch. Her name has been carried down through generations. As her namesake, Anaïs's grandmother is the oldest living witch in this lineage.

Because of Lilith witches live longer. Because of her they have a connection with the unseen world. Because of her witches must remain hidden.

If they were ever to reveal themselves, all the Adams would rise up and discount them. And all the Eves would support him. And not because they want to be on top. They would do it purely out of fear of the unknown, which he would exploit to spread the fear of having no control. When all along, the Eves should know, the universe is the only one in control.

Lilith and her witches are no threat. They are merely there to serve the universe.

THE ORACLE

Lilith guided Anaïs into the shade of the palm tree. She indicated the low stone wall. 'Take a seat, Anaïs.'

The witch did as instructed. Lilith sat next to her. She looked out at the surrounding trees. 'Welcome to my garden, Anaïs. Do you like it?'

The little witch nodded.

'Good.'

She took Anaïs by the hand again. Once more a warmth surged through the little witch's body, toasting her from the inside and causing her to feel slightly dizzy.

'You can relax, Anaïs,' said Lilith. 'You are safe here.'

The dizziness subsided. Anaïs followed Lilith's gaze into the garden. She glanced up above the tree tops at the hill she had just descended. Her thoughts went out to her companions. In the waters beyond the hill lay the Catamarine. She hoped this was still the case. 'I have people waiting for me. Shouldn't I go get them?'

'They'll be fine without you for a while.'

'But they're important to me.'

'I know, Anaïs,' said Lilith. She placed her other hand gently on the witch's chin. Cupping Anaïs's jaw in her hand, she gently turned her head in order to look her directly in the eye. 'Right now you are more important. You are not like them, Anaïs. In fact, you are unlike any other. Even other witches. You come from a long line of pure witches. Not the witches you know from the Organisation and the Brotherhood, but real witches.'

'I don't understand.' Anaïs knotted her brow. 'How can there be different sorts of witches? Aren't we all the same?'

'No.' Lilith shook her head. 'They are watered-down versions of us. You have powers they don't have. Special powers. You can do real magic.'

'Real magic?'

'Yes. Do you remember the volcano?'

Anaïs nodded. 'Of course, but how do you know about that?'

'My promptuary showed me. It shows me many things.' Lilith released Anaïs's jaw and hand. The warmth coursing through her began to dissipate. 'If you are to harness your full potential,' Lilith continued, 'you must become one with your handbook.'

Anaïs recalled how, in the crater of the volcano, the promptuary had become putty in her hands. 'I have done that already.'

'Yes, I'm sure you have, but only to some extent. To make full use of it you must understand where the power comes from.' Lilith laid her hand on Anaïs's chest. She felt a fresh surge of warmth flush her body. 'It comes from you and not the promptuary. It is merely a conduit—a tool. Although not the case with your handbook, many tools have handles for a reason. If you are the one holding it, you have to do the work. Without an artisan, a tool is an inanimate object.'

'I have felt that. The promptuary becoming part of me.'

'Good.' Lilith smiled. She removed her hand from Anaïs's chest and straightened in her seat. 'May I see it?'

'Of course.' Anaïs extracted the handbook from her beret. She laid it on her lap.

Lilith ran her finger over the contours of the star on the cover. The star responded, glowing brightly. 'You must also realise a tool has the potential to destroy as much as it has the ability to create. It is up to you how you use it. Use it with caution, Anaïs.'

Anaïs sighed. 'But I don't know if I can do any of this. Look at me. I'm a child.'

Lilith shook her head. 'Not true, Anaïs. That may well be how others perceive you, but you know yourself, you are no child.'

'I am,' protested Anaïs. 'Look at me. I'm stuck in this body. Why am I in it, anyway? Can't we do something about it? I don't want to be a girl. I want to be a woman. I want to grow up. Really grow up.'

'You are a woman,' said Lilith. 'Your physical form is immaterial, Anaïs. You need to come to terms with this. Some girls never grow up to be women no matter what they look like. You are not one of them. The mere fact you don't want this physical form is testament to that. Most people don't want to grow up.'

Anaïs dropped her gaze. She stared at the swathe of grass before her, its bright greenness starkly contrasting with the arid hill rising above the garden. 'Growing up means taking responsibility.'

'Partly.' Lilith pursed her lips. 'If you think back over your actions, you have already done that. You already know you have responsibilities far greater than anyone else. You have to stop comparing yourself to them. And that includes the body you have been given.'

'But can't we control it? Is there nothing we can do?'

'The universe will provide when it sees fit.'

Anaïs huffed. 'Sometimes I think the universe is a crock of crap.' She bit her lip and glanced warily at the sky, half expecting a thunderbolt to strike her down. 'Maybe I shouldn't have said that.'

Lilith grinned. 'The universe is used to being cursed. You will have to do better than that to get a reaction.'

Anaïs sighed. 'And what about the other witches? You know, the Organisation and the Brotherhood.'

'They fear you, Anaïs. They fear you because they cannot comprehend what you know. People always fear the unknown.'

'So I have to avoid them?'

'No, not necessarily. Some can help you. Others not. Beware of those who turn against you. Those who fear the unknown also try to destroy it.'

Anaïs drew in a deep breath and expelled it sharply. 'So who can I trust?'

'You will know,' said Lilith, her voice calm and

unwavering. 'If you search yourself, you will already know who is with you and who is against you.'

Anaïs fell silent. She raised her head and examined Lilith's face. The woman was extremely old. Her skin deeply creased—almost prune-like. Yet her eyes were bright and youthful. They had a playful glint to them as if she were a mischievous child up to no good.

'How old are you?'

'Anaïs!' Lilith flashed her eyes. 'It's rude to ask someone their age.'

The little witch shrugged. 'I'm just curious. You know, being a witch and all. I'd kind of like to know how old I could potentially become.'

Lilith scratched her chin thoughtfully. 'To be honest, I don't precisely know. I stopped counting at a thousand. That's actually the last time I celebrated a birthday. Then I gave up. I suppose that was about a century ago. Let's give it a ball-park figure. Eleven hundred has a nice ring to it.'

'Eleven hundred!' exclaimed Anaïs. 'Man! I couldn't imagine being that old. Getting to eighteen was bad enough.'

'Don't remind me,' said Lilith, rolling her eyes. 'Being a teenager is hell.'

'You remember that?'

'Of course! Who could forget being a teenager?'

Anaïs raised an eyebrow. 'That bad, eh?'

'Yes.' Lilith winked at her granddaughter. 'But don't worry. It's a passing phase. Although, unfortunately, it usually gets worse before it comes good again.'

'Great!'

Lilith adopted a serious tone. 'Trouble is coming, Anaïs.'

'I know.' Anaïs paused. She gnawed on her lower lip. 'I felt it. And I saw it. The shades.'

'You will have to deal with them.'

'Me?' Anaïs slid away from Lilith. Swivelling to face her grandmother, she pulled one leg up onto the stone seat. 'But what about you? You have all the knowledge. And the power. Or at least, you know how to use the power you have.'

'Yes I do, Anaïs. But I can't get involved. The knowledge I have is sacred. It is priceless. It is my duty to protect it. You need to think of me as a sort of library.'

'A library?'

'Yes,' said Lilith. 'I can only give advice. My days of roaming are over. You are always welcome to visit, but I must stay here. There are very few places on this planet where I am safe. This is one of them.'

'Safe?' Anaïs glanced warily at the trees encircling them. 'Are you in danger?'

'No, not exactly. No one can touch me here. This garden is protected. No one can get in.'

'Then how did I get in?'

Lilith shot a sly grin at the witch. 'I let you in.'

'But I don't want to go either,' said Anaïs mournfully. 'I want to stay here.'

'I'm sorry.' Lilith placed her warm hand on Anaïs's knee. 'You have much to do. You will have to leave.'

The older witch's touch flushed Anaïs's body again. Her head swam. 'I can't do it alone.'

'You don't have to. You have a very powerful ally. You only need to find her.'

'Her?'

'Yes, Anaïs,' said Lilith softly. 'Your mother.'

A TRINITY

Anaïs raised both eyebrows. 'My mother?'

'Yes,' said Lilith. 'You have met her recently.'

'Met her? My mother? Where? When?'

'You have met many times.' Lilith measured her words. 'She has never been far away. She is there to protect you. She is always looking out for you. But, as you know, we can never get too close to one another.'

Anaïs frowned. 'That's something I don't understand. If that's so, how is it possible that we can sit here—together?'

'I told you before. We are special—different to the others. For us there is an anomaly. The rule of being in close proximity doesn't apply. It skips a generation. As I am your grandmother, you and I can be together. Although, that is not to say we will not feel each other's auras.'

To demonstrate, Lilith removed her hand from Anaïs's knee. Almost at once, the hot flush running through the little witch subsided. More than before Anaïs felt her body temperature plummet. An involuntary shiver ran down her spine. She wrapped her arms around her torso, hugging herself. 'Brr …'

Lilith smiled sweetly. 'Sorry.'

Anaïs cleared her throat. 'But how could I even be born if I can't be near my mother?'

'We are all born as naturals. As a baby your powers were not as strong as they are now. Your mother did raise you up until a certain point. You would have been too young to remember. Usually a child's long-term memory only begins after the age of two. At which point your powers also began to grow at an exponential rate. Then you could no longer be near your mother.'

'So that is when I ended up with Nan?'

'Yes,' said Lilith. 'The Organisation took charge of you.'

'To protect me?'

'No, to protect themselves, Anaïs.' Lilith narrowed her eyes. 'I told you, there are those who fear you. They hoped to control you. It is far better to keep your enemies close. That way you can keep an eye on them.'

'Enemy? How am I an enemy?' Anaïs shook her head to clear it. 'This is way too much information all at once.'

'I understand.'

Anaïs took a deep breath. She expelled it loudly. 'Let me get this straight for a moment. If the Organisation took me in, they must have known who my mother was?'

'Oh yes, they knew,' said Lilith. 'They tried to hide

both yours and your mother's identities from your father.'

'Then Caput Mortuum lied to me.'

'Yes. Unfortunately, witches are not immune to acts of deception. Caput and Deus are in a power struggle. They have been for eons. You are their wild card. Whoever has control over you has the balance of power. Or, at least, that is how they see it.'

Anaïs scowled. 'But the Organisation failed to hide me. He found out who I was.'

'Yes. Your actions in Amsterdam, and then in Cornwall, exposed you to his son Ignatius. And, in turn, to his father—your father. That is why the Organisation tried to prevent you from taking action—to keep you cocooned. They would have preferred you remain in the dark, not only about him, but about who and what you are.'

Anaïs screwed up her face. She scratched the back of her head vigorously. 'This is all too weird. What am I, some kind of super weapon?'

Lilith chuckled. 'No, but you are a serious threat. As I said, you have powers they don't have. They want control. When they took you they even concealed your whereabouts from your mother.'

The little witch flashed her eyes. 'That's terrible.'

'Yes.' Lilith's expression darkened. 'No mother should ever be separated from her child.'

'But then, how did she find me?'

'Your name. You changed it. You used her name. And that summoned her.'

Anaïs scratched her head again. 'Her name is Anaïs Thistle?'

'No.'

'What is it then?'

Lilith paused. She dropped her eyes, staring at her hands lying in her lap.

Anaïs squirmed in her seat. 'Lilith?'

The witch raised her head. She looked deep into Anaïs's enquiring eyes. 'Siana Thistle.'

'Siana?'

'Yes. Not only are you physically connected, but also … in name. Your names are an emordnilap.'

'They're what?'

'Try spelling your name backwards.'

Anaïs closed her eyes and concentrated, reorganising the letters of her name in her head. She opened her eyes. 'Oh!'

Lilith gave her a knowing smile.

'Where is she now?'

'I expect she's out there looking for you,' said Lilith. 'However, she will have difficulty finding you. This time you made your escape too good. This is fortunate. If she can't find you, neither can they.'

'I suppose that's a good thing,' said Anaïs sullenly. 'You mentioned trouble is coming.'

'Trouble is already here, Anaïs.'

The little witch glanced around frantically. 'Where?'

'Not here. This island is uninhabited.' Lilith waved her hand towards the blue waters, visible above the tree line out in the bay. 'Out there.'

'The shades?'

Lilith nodded grimly. 'By sealing the volcanoes, you stopped access to hellhounds.'

'Why is that such a problem?'

'The shades are aware something has changed,' said the older witch quietly, almost as if she were afraid the dead would hear. 'Presently, it is not a huge problem. But it will become one.'

'When?'

'When the shades become aware of each other. As individuals they can do little harm. As a group, they can.'

'Why would they even do that?'

'There are shades who have unfinished business that should never be … well … finished.' She paused, considering the ramifications of her words. 'They are the rogues who can upset balance in the universe.'

'How do we stop them?'

'It is in your hands, Anaïs. Only you can restore the balance. But, you must be aware, sacrifices will need to be made.'

'Sacrifices?'

'As with all witches, you are sworn to protect naturals. A time will come when to protect those around you, you will need to go it alone. You must make certain the shades are hidden from themselves.'

'You mean I will need to get back the hellhounds?'

'No, I think not.' Lilith shook her head emphatically. 'Hellhounds are a blunt instrument. You can pound away all you like with them, but you won't solve the problem.'

'What will solve the problem?'

'You,' said Lilith.

Anaïs raised an eyebrow. 'Me?'

'And your mother. Together you have the power to stop this.'

'How?'

'When the time is right you will know.'

Anaïs snorted in exasperation. 'You're not very helpful.'

'Find your mother, Anaïs. That's the only advice I can give.'

Confronted with the enormity of her task, the little witch's voice wavered. 'But how do I find her?'

'You have all the tools you need. I told you before, you only need to use them properly.'

Anaïs slapped her palm on her forehead in frustration. An object dropped from the tree above her onto her hand. Feeling the weight of it she shook her hand to flick it off. It remained stuck to it. Anaïs brought her hand down in front of her. On it was the largest ladybird she had ever seem. It was practically the size of her hand. 'Ew!'

'This is a gift from me, Anaïs.'

'A gift?'

Lilith nodded.

Anaïs eyed the insect dubiously. 'Will it help me find my mother?'

The older witch shook her head. 'No, but if you ever need me, tell the ladybird.'

'Does it have a name?'

'Only if you give it one.'

'A name?' Anaïs thought for a moment. 'I know. We're in Greece. I think I'll call her Sappho.'

'A good choice.'

Gingerly, Anaïs raised her hand and brought the insect closer to her face. It was beautiful. The spots on its back shimmered in the sunlight. *Are they moving?* Anaïs blinked and refocussed. *Yes, they are.* The spots zipped around in a circle and reconfigured themselves. They morphed to form a face.

Startled, Anaïs's jaw dropped. 'Ahem …' She looked at Lilith.

The witch grinned. She nodded at the ladybird. 'She likes you. Introduce yourself.'

The little witch cleared her throat. 'Hello, Sappho. My name is Anaïs.'

The eyes in the face blinked.

'It's time you returned to your friends, Anaïs,' said Lilith. 'You have much to do.'

Keeping a wary eye on the ladybird, Anaïs glanced sideways at the witch. 'Will I see you again?'

'Most certainly.'

Anaïs stood. Lilith did the same. Wordlessly, she drew Anaïs into her arms. The hot flush returned. Anaïs bathed in its warmth. The witch released Anaïs from her embrace. She held her at arm's length by the shoulders. Anaïs gazed up into the Lilith's eyes. A calm swept over her. A reassuring feeling that somehow, even with the gravity of her predicament, eventually all would be fine.

Anaïs sniffed. 'You don't know what this means to finally meet you, Lilith. Or should I call you grandmother?'

'Lilith is perfectly fine.'

Anaïs smiled. 'It's such a relief to know I have family. Real family that I can trust.'

'I understand. It has been difficult for me too, Anaïs. Not being able to contact you.' A pained expression momentarily clouded Lilith's face. She brightened, smiling sweetly at her granddaughter. 'I wish you well. One day soon we will see each other again. When you find her, please give my love to your mother.' She took her hands off Anaïs's shoulders and let them drop by her side.

'I will.' Reluctantly, Anaïs stepped away from Lilith. She turned. Slowly she walked across the clearing and stepped onto a path between the trees. Sappho flew from her hand and alighted on her shoulder. Anaïs stopped and glanced at the ladybird. She turned to bid Lilith a final farewell.

The clearing and palm tree were no longer visible. The trees surrounding it had transformed. Thick and gnarled—a mesh of trunks, branches and leaves—they provided a natural barrier of defence against prying eyes.

Anaïs's heart sank. To her disappointment, her grandmother had vanished.

RAINBOW

Anaïs left the confines of the garden and the ruined town behind her. She began the steep climb up the hill. Her mind ran over the conversation with Lilith.

How am I going to find my mother? She said I have the tools. But which tool?

Anaïs stopped. She removed her beret and stared into it. *Whatever I need must be in here.* The beret was a black hole, revealing nothing. Anaïs sighed. *What do I need?*

She cleared her head. Focusing on the question, she reached cautiously into the hat. She felt around in the cavernous abyss. Strangely, the beret was devoid of its usual jumbled mess of contents. She felt nothing. 'C'mon!' she cried out in frustration.

She took a moment to compose herself. 'You can do this. Concentrate!'

Anaïs closed her eyes. She breathed in deeply through her nostrils. *Give me what I need to find my mother.*

A heavy object sprang into her hand so hard it jarred her entire arm. She held it securely. The object's substantial mass weighed heavily on her arm. She frowned. 'What do I have that is so heavy?'

Struggling with the weight, she extracted her hand. In her grip was the promptuary. She flipped the beret onto her head and slapped her forehead. 'Duh!' she cried.

The gesture alarmed the ladybird. Sappho flew into the air. She circled the witch before repositioning herself on Anaïs's shoulder.

'Sorry, Sappho. My bad.'

The insect fluttered its wings in response.

Anaïs looked at her handbook and frowned again. 'Why are you so heavy all of a sudden? Was it Lilith? Did she give you more information? More knowledge?'

The star on the promptuary glowed brightly and then steadily began to pulse. Anaïs shrugged. She opened the book. 'Show me my mother. Show me Siana Thistle.'

A rainbow spewed forth from the join between the pages. It shot up into the sky.

The shock of the apparition caused Anaïs to drop the handbook at her feet. She stumbled backwards and fell, jarring her coccyx. She scrambled to her knees, massaging her rear end. Tilting her head, she stared up in wonder at the rainbow. She squinted, following the pathway the ribbon of colours created.

Unlike a normal rainbow it did not arc back to the earth but formed a solid wall. Narrow at its base, rising perfectly perpendicular to the book, it fanned out above her, filling the sky. The colours within it swirled—constantly changing, refracting light like a kaleidoscope—flowing one over another. The rainbow's solid cliff-like structure was short-lived. It disintegrated, splintering into a massive cloud of tiny coloured shards.

Speechless at the sight, Anaïs squatted. Her mouth agape, she sat down on her ankles and hugged her knees.

The small multicoloured shards fused together into larger objects, forming oblong pebble-like shapes. The oval forms emitted their own sources of light. Sparkling like fireflies, the forms transformed further. They sprouted wings, adding to their firefly appearance. Anaïs's eyes widened. Recovering from her initial shock, she narrowed her eyes and peered closely at the shapes. They were not fireflies but another insect altogether. Floating above her were thousands of multi-coloured butterflies.

Bunching into a solitary group they dove. Twisting and spiralling like a flock of sparrows, they snaked through the air before configuring themselves into an enormous egg shape.

The butterflies hovered directly above Anaïs. Assembling themselves into distinct colours they began to portray the contours of a face. First eyes appeared, then cheekbones, a nose, and finally lips. The lips parted. The smile which followed had such warmth Anaïs's heart skipped a beat.

Anaïs recognised the face immediately. It was the face of the woman from Amsterdam. The same woman who had caused the death of Nan. The same woman who had been perched on the basilica in Barcelona. The woman she now knew in her heart to be Siana Thistle—her mother.

Anaïs stared deep into her eyes. Eyes which were the deepest shade of purple. A sudden flash of light momentarily blinded her. Her vision blurred. She blinked to bring it into focus.

Slowly her sight returned. However, the image she saw was not what she expected. Her surroundings had changed. She was surprised to find herself no longer on the island, but in a small room.

She glanced down at her body. She had shrunk in size. She gasped. *What the—? What twisted magic is this? I just grew!* Completely transformed—now a toddler wrapped snugly in a thick blanket— she sat in a child's stroller. Her heart pounded. *Please don't let this be real! I don't want to go back to that!*

She raised her head. Before her stood Siana Thistle. Her mother bent forward, bringing her face close to Anaïs's. Reaching down, she went to adjust the blanket wrapped around her daughter.

An arc of static electricity snapped between them, producing a loud crackling sound. Anaïs felt herself fly backwards. Time slowed. She watched with a mixture of fascination and horror as her mother flew across the room in the opposite direction. Siana crashed through a window on the far side of the room. The thin wooden muntins holding the four panes of glass splintered easily with the force of her flight. The panes themselves also shattered. Her mother disappeared in a cloud of splintered glass.

Still cocooned in her stroller, Anaïs smashed into the wall behind her. The impact took the wind out of her. She blinked involuntarily. In an instant, with the blink, the room dematerialised and she was back on the island.

Above her the butterflies dispersed, exploding like a firework. The image of her mother's face vanished. The butterflies fell as sparks—glowing embers which rained down around her in a shower of colour. They hissed as they hit the ground.

From where the sparks landed, stalks sprouted from the earth. The bare twigs quickly developed into fully fledged plants—flowers with delicate petals. Anaïs stared in awe at the carpet of wildflowers surrounding her. Their beauty took her breath away.

'Wow!' she exclaimed.

She glanced down at her handbook lying open on the ground in front of her. Its pages flapped innocently in the wind, looking for all the world like any ordinary book. She scooped up her promptuary, closed it and held it to her chest.

She shook her head and muttered under her breath. 'You are truly amazing.'

THE WAVE

The entire experience of meeting Lilith, as well as the revelations about her mother, had taken their toll. Anaïs felt both physically and mentally drained. She stood, took off her beret and dropped the promptuary into it. She replaced the hat upon her head and pulled it down snug over her ears.

She dragged her body up the slope. On the pinnacle of the hill she collapsed on a rock. Its jagged edges dug into her skin. She barely felt it, her body numb. She ran her hand over the rock's surface. It had pits and gouges like a golf ball. She mused that perhaps it had once been a meteorite.

Where have you been? And what have you seen? She grinned. *I doubt you've ever seen what I've seen.*

She looked down into the bay. The Catamarine floated serenely in the calm blue waters. On deck, next to the wheelhouse, a figure waved at her. She screwed up her eyes and peered at it. It was the Apothecary. Anaïs waved back.

The Apothecary continued to wave. She pointed at the sky. *What now?*

Anaïs raised her head. To the west, beyond the Catamarine, ominous dark clouds had formed. What caught her eye was not only the darkness of the clouds, but also the sea beneath them. It was practically pitch black except for a single white line. The line ran along the horizon, dividing the water from the sky.

Anaïs shielded her eyes. Creating makeshift binoculars around them with her hands, she focussed on the horizon. The white line did not maintain constant proportions. Erratically, it swelled and contracted. Not only did it fluctuate in this way, it also appeared to be gradually thickening as a whole.

As it grew, it became clear to Anaïs what the line was. At first she thought it was the peaks of a series of waves. However, on closer inspection, it was not a series of waves but a single enormous one. Anaïs dropped her hands in her lap. Stretching across the entire width of the horizon, the wave was heading towards her.

She turned her attention to the Apothecary. Ella was jumping up and down on the deck, waving her arms around frantically.

'Oh!' said Anaïs, realising what was going on.

It was obvious why the Apothecary was gesticulating. Ella was clearly beside herself. She was not greeting her; she was urging her to return to the vessel. And fast.

Anaïs frowned. The waters in the bay seemed to be draining. To her horror she watched as more of the shoreline at the base of the hill became exposed.

She pushed her feelings of exhaustion aside.

Jumping to her feet, she eyed the slope of the hill stretching out below her. *How the heck did I get up here?* She saw no pathway, only what appeared to be one large rockslide. She glanced up at the oncoming wave. It had increased further in size. *No time. Just go. Even if you have to roll to the bottom.*

A movement on her shoulder caught Anaïs's attention. Sappho fluttered her wings. Anaïs glanced at the steep slope running down to the shore. *What am I going to do with you? Think, you idiot!* She let out a loud puff of air. *Got it!* She held her coat pocket open. 'Quick, Sappho, get in here. You'll be safe … I hope.'

The ladybird did as requested. She scuttled down the witch's arm and into the pocket.

'Right!' Anaïs took a deep breath and focussed on her objective. 'Let's do this!'

She shoved herself off the rock and launched herself down the slope. She ran for all she was worth. Slipping and sliding on the loose stones on the hillside, she fought to maintain her balance. She fell more than she ran. However, the momentum of her slightly grounded free-fall carried her forward and kept her upright. When she felt herself falling she pushed herself off nearby boulders. Trying desperately to stay vertical, and keep a tenuous grip on the ground beneath her, she pumped her legs harder to keep them under her body.

Even so, she lost her footing. Her legs went out from under her. She crashed down heavily on her side. She felt the scrape of the rough surface under the palm of her hand as she attempted to steady herself. Ignoring the pain, she shoved herself back to her feet.

She glanced down at the foot of the hill. The shoreline was getting closer now. Or was it? The water in the bay seemed to have receded even more, the undertow of the approaching wave sucking it up. It exposed the stone pathway she had taken to get ashore. Anaïs half-grinned. *That's fortunate.*

Within moments she reached the foot of the hill. She sprinted across the narrow stone causeway, her eyes fixed on her target. The ship's deck was now deserted. As she approached it she heard the Catamarine's engine gun. Then it was drowned out by an almighty roar. Glancing sideways she stared with a mixture of horror and awe at the wave. It towered several storeys high, blocking out half the sky.

She lunged over the small gap between the stone causeway and the vessel. Diving under the railing, she slid across the smooth deck on her stomach. She clambered to her feet, took two steps towards the door and jumped inside. She stumbled and fell, sprawling out on the floor. She heard the door slam behind her.

Rolling onto her back, Anaïs saw the librarian standing next to the entrance. Irritatingly, she was tapping her foot. Even through terror-filled her eyes, Immi still managed to fire off a snide remark. 'Nice of you to join us,' she snapped.

ON BOARD

Ella worked furiously at the console. Flipping a series of switches, she punched the submerge button. Immediately water began to wash over the hull and against the windows as the vessel descended.

'What's going on?' asked Anaïs.

'You saw, it didn't you?'

'The wave, you mean? Yes.'

'It's a tsunami,' said Ella. She indicated a set of three Bakelite dials mounted under the main console. 'I found an old radio and managed to dial into a shipping broadcast. There's huge panic out there.' She waved her hand at the ceiling. 'It seems that little eruption we had on Sicily is causing widespread carnage. Everybody thinks Armageddon is upon us.'

'We have a radio?' Anaïs knotted her brow. 'Wait! Armageddon?'

'Yeah, the smoke from the volcano has blacked out the sun in Italy. A piece of the mountain broke off and slid into the sea, causing the wave. The wave hit the west coast of Italy. Now it's heading this way. They are predicting more of them.'

'Oops!' said Anaïs. She covered her mouth with her hand. *What have I done?*

'That's an understatement,' said Ella.

'And now?'

'We have to get under the wave, otherwise we'll be swept up with it.' Ella eyed the dials on the console. 'If that happens, who knows where we'll end up. Most probably on top of a hill somewhere.'

'Oh!'

'There's a lot of islands here in the Cyclades, so that should provide some form of protection. But there's no telling what will happen.'

No longer able to contain herself, the librarian interrupted the conversation. Enraged, she spat at Anaïs. 'Why did you take off like that? We couldn't get in contact with you.'

'Sorry,' said Anaïs meekly.

'Why were you gone so long?'

'I wasn't gone that long,' protested Anaïs.

'Yes!' cried Immi, infuriated. 'Yes, you were! You were gone for a day.'

'A day!' Anaïs shook her head. 'It was only a couple of hours.'

'No.' The librarian returned the gesture, shaking her head vigorously. 'It was definitely a day. You know, that cycle of twenty-four hours when the sun goes down and comes up again?'

Anaïs rolled her eyes.

'That happened,' continued Immi. 'How could you miss a day? Were you asleep or something?'

'No, I was with my grandmother.'

'What?' Immi wrinkled her brow. 'Your grandmother?'

'Yes.' Anaïs was confused. *Did time stop for me in the garden?* She cast the thought aside. There were more pressing problems. 'Shouldn't we worry less about where I was and more about getting safe?'

The librarian glanced out the window at the churning waters and relented. 'You're right.'

Ella slumped in her chair. 'I think we'll be okay now. But we should get away from the island to be sure. Do you have any idea where we go next?'

'Possibly. Let me have a look.' Anaïs took out her promptuary and opened the book. 'Show me the location of Siana Thistle.'

'Who's Siana Thistle?' exclaimed Immi.

'My mother.'

'Mother? I didn't think you had a mother.'

'Everyone has a mother, you dope,' said Anaïs, screwing up her face. 'My grandmother told me about her. I think she can help. But I will need to find her.'

The promptuary produced a three-dimensional image of southern Europe. In the centre a purple dot winked on and off. 'Where is that?'

Ella leaned over the arm of her chair. She scrutinised the map. 'A little to the north. Not far from here.'

'Zoom in,' said Anaïs.

The promptuary obliged.

Anaïs rubbed her eyebrow. 'There's nothing there. It's in the middle of the ocean.'

'There must be something there,' said Ella. 'Maybe a really small island.'

'Maybe.'

Warning lights began flashing on the console and a klaxon sounded. The deck suddenly lifted. The entire vessel tilted to one side, throwing them all off balance. Ella gripped the arms of her chair and managed to stay in it. Anaïs stumbled across the deck and collided with Immi. The librarian cried out in pain as the witch's elbow dug into her ribs. The collision sent her careening further across the deck and into the wall.

'Quick, Anaïs!' screamed Ella. 'Your promptuary. Put it on the console. We have to get out of here.'

Under the influence of the tide, the vessel surged once more. Anaïs dropped to her knees and crawled across the floor to the console. She secured the book to its fasteners. Ella reached forward and hit the green button. The craft responded immediately, shooting them forward. As it gained momentum, it steadied.

~

On the surface the ferocity of the wave was enormous. It crashed into the rocky slopes of the island's shore. With it came all manner of objects, some of them carried all the way from Italy. A small fishing boat, part of a cruise liner, the wall of a prefabricated house and a blue Portaloo all deposited themselves on the shore.

The steep slopes of Delos broke the back of the

wave. It swirled around the island, leaving much of the lee side unscathed, including the ruins of the ancient town and Lilith's garden.

Further to the north and south the many islands of the Cyclades further dispersed the wave. By the time it reached the shores of Turkey much of its strength had been depleted.

The damage it left in its wake was tremendous. In years to come, many would recall the freak waves which had left their mark on the Mediterranean.

A certain little witch would never forget it.

REVELATION

The Apothecary had her eyes firmly fixed on the Catamarine's instruments.

'I think we will be safe now,' she said. 'But we will have to stay submerged until this passes.'

'Any idea how long that will take?' enquired Anaïs.

Ella pursed her lips. 'No, I'm not a seismologist. Can't your handbook predict stuff like that?'

'I'm not sure. I never tried.'

'Oh!' said Ella. 'Before I forget. I don't know if this is important, but in all the panic I forgot to mention something. There was other news on the radio.'

Anaïs raised an eyebrow. 'Other news?'

'Yeah, something weird happened on TV.'

'Weird?'

'Yes,' said Ella. 'But you can never be sure if it's for real. There's so much fabrication in the media. It could be a hoax.'

'What happened?'

Ella took her eyes off the console and looked at Anaïs. 'John Lennon appeared in a TV interview.'

'Why is that so strange? People appear on TV all the time. Who is John Lennon?'

'One of the Beatles.' Ella frowned. 'How come you don't know that?'

Anaïs returned the gesture. 'Since when do naturals communicate with insects? And, for that matter, give them names?' She paused, realising she had done the exact same thing with Sappho. She slid her hand down over her jacket and felt for a lump. Reassuringly, she felt the insect stir in her pocket. *Whew! Thank goodness she's still okay.*

'They don't,' said Ella. 'Well, I suppose they do occasionally. But that's beside the point. The Beatles were a rock group. A band. Musicians. They were famous in the 1960s and 70s.'

Anaïs shrugged. 'Before my time.'

'They were huge. They're still famous now.' Ella raised an eyebrow. 'How come you don't know who they are? Everybody knows the Beatles.'

'Ella,' said Anaïs, 'I may be a witch but I don't know everything. Besides, I don't get out much.' She considered what she had said for a moment. 'Well, that used to be the case. Now it seems to be the only thing I do.' She glanced around the wheelhouse. 'Anyway, I don't get what's so weird about a musician appearing on TV. Doesn't that happen all the time?'

Ella bent forward to get Anaïs's full attention. She looked the little witch directly in the eyes. 'John Lennon is dead, Anaïs.'

Anaïs paled. 'Are you sure?'

'Yes,' said Ella, slowly nodding. 'I'm very sure about that.'

Anaïs gnawed on her lower lip. *Not good. Not good at all.* She drew in a deep breath. 'You better show me this John what's-his-name.'

'John Lennon.' Ella cocked her head at the object fastened to the console. 'Why don't you ask your promptuary?'

'Don't you need it to set the Catamarine's course?'

'Already done that,' said Ella. 'You can remove it.'

Anaïs unfastened her handbook. She requested details about John Lennon. The holographic image of the map showing the course to their destination disappeared. The promptuary's open pages flashed before going dark. It momentarily displayed a black slate before lighting up. It then began playing back short snapshots of live footage. It showed the Beatles performing. Following this it scrolled through stills of the band's history, including a meeting with Elvis Presley, ending with the death of John Lennon in New York.

The promptuary flipped through the front pages of the world's major newspapers at the time. All their headlines proclaimed the same notice: John Lennon Shot Dead. The handbook displayed a final image of an obituary. It zoomed in, showing a close-up of his face.

Anaïs gulped. Her face turned white.

Ella watched her reaction. 'Are you all right, Anaïs?'

'I'm not sure.'

'What's the problem? You look like you've seen a ghost.'

'I have.' Anaïs studied his features, particularly noting his thick-lensed glasses. 'I think I've met him.'

'Met him?'

'Yes. He pestered me on the street in Amsterdam,' said Anaïs. 'Something about a woman. He wrote her name on the footpath.' She scratched her head. *What was her name?* She sniffed. 'Now I think about it, I'm pretty sure I saw him in London too. He also appeared at the airport in Barcelona. Since then I haven't seen him again. I thought I'd gotten rid of him.'

'Well,' said Ella. 'You may have gotten rid of him, but that doesn't mean he's not still around. That is, if it's really the person you saw. Maybe we should find the TV interview?'

'Maybe.' The little witch instructed the promptuary to search for the last known appearance of John Lennon.

The promptuary did as instructed. It flashed up a multitude of images, flipping through them like a set of playing cards. Eventually it settled on a solitary image. It expanded the image, projecting it as a large framed picture hovering above the handbook's open pages.

Static ran through the image. There was a crackling sound, then the still began to move. It depicted the head of a man. There was something incredibly false about him. Everything was too perfect. He was so pristinely manicured, he looked more like a store mannequin than a human being. This was emphasised by the heavy makeup he was wearing which limited his facial expressions. His black hair was slicked tight across his skull. More akin to a helmet than a head of hair, it contributed to his robot-like appearance.

The man was listening intently to someone. Off camera a voice began to speak. 'Hell! I wouldn't even put it past them to instigate natural disasters.'

The helmet-headed man tilted his head to one side. 'Who?'

The camera flipped to a shot of another man. This one wore coke-bottle glasses. Anaïs sucked in her breath at the sight of him.

'The witches,' said John Lennon.

The robot man, apparently the presenter of the talk-show, was not the only one with an odd appearance. The shade's camouflage flickered on and off like a bad broadcast signal. It switched between his disguise and revealing the face of the real John Lennon beneath it. The only constant being the thick-lensed glasses.

'How do you know any of this?' enquired the presenter, seemingly unperturbed by the shades changing appearance. 'Have you ever met one?'

'Yes.' John nodded, the flickering camouflage making his movements jerky. 'I've met one of them a few times. She refused to help me.' He paused to inhale deeply. The studio's microphones picked up the sound of air through his nostrils, yet his chest showed no movement. 'This might seem a bit odd, but she was an older woman disguised in the body of a child.'

'So, if I have this right …' The presenter furrowed his brow deeply, cracking his makeup. 'These witches are similar to how you described the dead. Both they and you all have some kind of disguise to hide their true identities.'

The camera panned out, revealing both men seated opposite one another on sofas in a large television studio.

'Yes,' said the flickering image of John Lennon.

The host rubbed his chin. 'This interviewer, for one, is very sceptical.'

Lennon held up one hand and, with the other, pointed at its flickering form. 'I would think this would be proof enough for you, mate,' he said dryly.

'Mmm … That could be a simple magic trick. You wouldn't believe what people try to pull on this show.' The presenter adjusted his tie. He cleared his throat. 'But, for the moment, I will give you the benefit of the doubt. This …' He waved his hands at the shade's face. 'This strange disguise is one thing, but we would need some proof. One fact might dispel our doubts about the other things you've said. I'm sure our audience are much more interested in your first claim.' He turned to face the studio audience. 'Aren't we?'

The audience, whipped up by the warm-up comic, yelled and applauded.

The host cracked a sly smile. 'Well then, if you really are John Lennon, how do we know for sure?'

'I suppose I would have to reveal something personal about myself that very few people know,' said the shade.

'Yes,' said the host, adopting a serious tone. 'But then someone would have to verify your information. Considering you're … er … dead, that might be a bit difficult.'

'Maybe my mother could help.'

'Your mother?' The host straightened his posture. 'Perhaps sharing her name with us would be enough to verify who you are. What is it?'

'Her name is Julia,' said John.

On the deck of the Catamarine Anaïs gulped. *That was the name!*

John continued, 'Naturally, with a little digging, anyone would know that.'

'I was going to say the same thing,' replied the presenter. 'Then perhaps we need Julia to verify who you are. However, that may be a bit difficult. I doubt she's still alive.'

'No, sadly, she isn't.' For a moment the shade appeared distressed by the information. Then he brightened. 'But I've found her.'

'You've found her!' The presenter's eyes widened. 'Is she here?'

'Yes,' said John stoically.

The presenter turned his focus to the studio audience. He smiled mischievously. 'Do you want to see her?'

The audience responded with loud cheering.

'Where is she, John?'

The shade pointed across the studio. The camera panned, following where he indicated. In the aisle between the edge of the stage and the first row of audience seating stood a young man. He was barely visible in the dim light.

The interviewer beckoned him to come forward.

The young man stepped up onto the stage and into the harsh studio lighting.

The interviewer frowned. 'But that's a man.'

'No it's not. Watch and wait,' said Lennon.

The camouflage cloaking the young man flickered and dematerialised, revealing a woman dressed in 1950s attire. She wore a floral dress fluffed out by an innumerable number of petticoats. Her facial features were strikingly similar to those of the shade's.

The audience gasped and drew in their collective breath.

'You see,' said John with a sense of proud achievement. 'I'm not the only one. We walk among you.'

Off-camera came the sound of a scuffle in the studio. The active camera shook, rocking the televised image from side to side. A man rushed into the frame. Lennon stood. He raised his hands defensively. Waving them frantically he yelled at the camera, 'No, stop! You must listen. There's nothing to be afraid of. We're all the same. We should—'

His final words were cut off as the broadcast was interrupted. On the Catamarine the frame above the promptuary went blank.

EXPOSURE

Let us pause for a moment. I mentioned at the very beginning that steps were put into place to control shade behaviour. Let me refresh your memory.

Although not the only occurrence of this in history, the black death was the worst time for shade activity. The dead outnumbered the living many-fold. As chaos abounded there was very little naturals could do to control them. That was when witches stepped in and the shade camouflage was created.

These disguises were thought to be indestructible. But, as a wise person once said to me, 'You know what "I think" did. It just thought. It didn't do anything remotely useful.' The universe is constantly in flux. Nothing lasts forever.

An occasional occurrence of a shade revealing itself to a natural can do no great harm. Almost everybody has a ghost story to tell. However, if shades become aware of their standing in the world—that they share it with naturals and are not completely isolated—then all hell breaks loose. Which, as is now disturbingly obvious, has already happened.

The real problem is that this phenomenon is entirely new to the modern witch community. Unfortunately, the shade camouflage was put into service long before any of the current witches were around. Except, perhaps, Lilith. However, what Lilith knows is anybody's guess. She's not exactly forthcoming with a great deal of information. We can assume she was also not party to the secret. This leaves us with a major quandary: How do you repair something when the knowledge of it is lost in the eons of time?

Another pressing question is: Why were these camouflages put into service in the first place?

There was a time when balance in the universe was in order. The dead lived alongside the living. The lines of communication were open. Witches were the conduit. They were revered and much sought after for their talents. No matter its size, every community had one. They went under various names: oracles, soothsayers, prophets, sages and fortune tellers. Their task, however, remained the same: listen to what the dead had to say and pass this on to the living.

Shades are libraries of knowledge. No matter who you are, as a natural, contacting your ancestors is of paramount importance. It is their experience that guides the future. Only through their enormous grasp and understanding of information can sensible advice be taken on a pertinent course of action. Knowledge of the past is fundamental to the future.

The ancients knew this. They used it to its full potential. In some cultures, as in the case of the Egyptians, the dead were honoured. Huge monuments were built to house them. They were protected. The dead were trusted for the advice they could give. In turn, witches were entrusted with the task of communicating with them.

Unfortunately, not all shades are equal.

As the Earth's population exploded, so did the shade populace. In the past, shades knew their place. They kept to themselves and only appeared at the request of a witch. This changed. They took communication into their own hands. It became a free-for-all.

Every shade had a story to tell. They forced themselves out into the open. Many bypassed witches altogether. The liberties they took created confusion. No one knew any more what advice was right or wrong.

Having the ability to communicate easily is not necessarily a good thing. This is as true in the natural world as in the supernatural. The current situation with the explosion of electronic communication, with underwater cables linking the entire world, is a prime example. The important messages became lost in a sea of chitter-chatter. They became watered down, the true knowledge obscured by legions of useless information.

Witches had no choice but to change the landscape. All control over shade activity had been lost. They were forced to step in and create a filter.

At this point the camouflage was created.

This completely shut the door to all communication between the living and the dead. It was a bold move on the part of witches, but a necessity. Control had to be maintained. Balance had to be restored.

However, it came at great cost. It was detrimental to the way witches were perceived. Some more astute naturals understood the importance of their action. They maintained their contact with witches and continued to honour their abilities. Disappointingly, the majority of naturals did not share this point of view.

To the greater populace it was perceived as an affront.

Although this window between worlds had only been open for a short period, many had become used to it. They felt their rights had been infringed upon. In their view everyone should have access to the dead. Witches had taken liberties with their special gifts. At no point had there been a discussion between them and naturals over a course of action. Naturals felt witches had sent the universe into disarray.

The end result: witches were shunned.

Forced to protect themselves, they went into hiding. They formed a closed community to enable them to continue their work. Only in small pockets of the world, where their true nature was still understood and revered, were they able to communicate freely with naturals. Only in these places, where the lines to the ancients were still strong, could witches rely on the protection and freedom they required. For the rest of the planet witchdom, as it had existed historically, ceased to exist.

The shade dilemma which Anaïs is now experiencing is not new. It is only one of many such occurrences. As with all things in the universe, cycles prevail. The universe has a habit of repeating itself. Irritatingly, no one knows precisely when this will occur. Thankfully witches, with their knowledge, can foresee this and can influence this pattern. In most cases witches have managed to reset the clock.

It remains to be seen if this will now be the case.

We can only hope that a certain little witch has a finger magical enough to insert into the clock face and reset the hour hand.

SAPPHO

Anaïs stared blankly at the empty frame above the promptuary. Her face pale, she let out a long sigh and leaned forward. Setting her elbows on the console, she put her head in her hands.

Sappho crawled out of her temporary pouch and walked up the witch's back. She sat on her shoulder and flexed her elytra.

The movement drew Ella's attention from the blank display. She glanced at Anaïs leaning over the console beside her and at the apparition which had appeared on her shoulder. Shrinking back in shock, she scrambled unsuccessfully to escape the confines of her chair, trying in vain to put some distance between her and the insect. 'Holy crap! What's that?'

'What?' said Anaïs, her voice muffled by her hands.

'That thing on your shoulder.'

Anaïs stood and turned her head. 'Oh, that? *She* is Sappho.'

'She? Sappho? So witches do name their insects?'

Anaïs smiled weakly. 'I guess so. She was a gift from my grandmother. She's special.' She took the insect from her shoulder and set it on the console. The spots on Sappho's back configured themselves into a broad grin. A pair of eyes appeared above the grin. The eyes blinked at Ella.

'That's freaky!'

'I think she's kind of cute,' said Anaïs.

Ella screwed up her nose. 'I don't know that I would describe it like that. Why is it grinning at me?'

'I suppose she likes you.'

Ella eyed the insect dubiously. 'I can't say the feeling is mutual. Sorry, but I have a slight aversion to bugs. Especially big ones.'

Anaïs turned to face the Apothecary. Her face grim, she measured her words. 'Right now, Ella, Sappho is not important. We have a huge problem. If the world believes what this Lennon guy just said and did, we are all in danger. How he managed to find, let alone communicate with, another shade, I have no idea. They can't do that.'

'Well, it was pretty convincing.' Ella shrugged. 'Although I have my doubts it was real. You see all kinds of things broadcast nowadays which turn out to be false. I've stopped watching stuff altogether.'

'It was real, Ella,' said Anaïs, her complexion ashen.

'Then it's a problem. If people believe he really is John Lennon, then they will believe what he says.'

'It's more than just a problem,' said Anaïs

mournfully. 'It's a disaster.' She slowly shook her head. 'What are we going to do?'

'Maybe she can help.'

'Who?'

'Your bug. You said she was special.'

Anaïs took her eyes off Ella. She assessed Sappho. 'Maybe,' she muttered reservedly.

One eye on the ladybird's back winked at her. The colour which had drained from the witch's face slowly returned. She brightened.

'Perhaps you're right, Ella.'

Anaïs slipped her hand under Sappho and cupped her in her palms. A surge of energy emanated from the insect. It sent a warmth rushing through the witch's body. The smile formed by the dots on her wings was infectious. A wide grin split Anaïs's face. She let her shoulders slump, a joyous wave of peace and contentment sweeping over her. Every fibre in her body tingled. She closed her eyes. The image of the grinning ladybird swam in her subconscious.

Sappho opened her elytra and unfurled her wings. They were translucent and shimmered. Spreading out wide from her thorax, they quadrupled her size. Specks of purple dust rose from her wing tips and floated around the wheelhouse. They twinkled like stars. Ella slid out of her chair, moved around it and took a tentative step away from the witch. She glanced enquiringly at Immi.

'Don't look at me for answers,' muttered the librarian sourly. With irritation, she swatted the glittering dust particles floating around her face. 'I know as much as you do.'

With her eyes closed and oblivious to what was going on around her, Anaïs sent out her thoughts to her grandmother. *'Lilith? Are you there?'*

Unbeknownst to Anaïs, Sappho folded her wings and closed her elytra. The spots on it reconfigured themselves. Lilith's face appeared in great detail. Ella and Immi watched the transformation with a mixture of apprehension and amazement.

Lilith's reassuring voice permeated Anaïs's head. Although Anaïs could not see them, the lips of the face formed on Sappho's elytra mouthed her words. *'Yes, Anaïs. I am here.'*

'The shades—'

'I know,' replied Lilith. *'I warned you trouble was coming.'*

'Trouble is a bit of an understatement. What can we do?'

'You will have to bide your time, Anaïs. For now, as witches, we are safe. The key is not to expose yourself. Once that happens, as history has taught us, naturals will rise against us. They always destroy what they fear.'

'But what about the shades?' enquired Anaïs. *'Now they are exposed. They will not be safe. Isn't it our job to help them?'*

'Indeed it is, Anaïs.'

'So, what do I do?'

'Stay the course, Anaïs. Find your mother.'

'That's it?'

'Yes.'

'But Lilith—'

'At the moment this is all the advice I can give. The future is

undefined, Anaïs. I cannot predict it. I can only tell you what I feel to be right. You should do the same. Use your intuition. It is one of your greatest gifts.'

Anaïs sighed. She opened her eyes. They widened. She drew her breath in sharply at the sight of Lilith's face configured on Sappho's back, nearly dropping her. The face gave her a reassuring smile. Opening her elytra again, Sappho unfurled her wings and fluttered them. Once more a cloud of sparkling purple dust filled the cabin. Awestruck, Anaïs stared at the spectacle. Sappho flapped her wings, lifted into the air and dropped down onto the console. The ladybird retracted her wings and closed the elytra covering them. Reconfiguring her spots, Sappho's eyes returned. They blinked.

Immi smirked and applauded. 'Great show!'

The librarian's reaction snapped Anaïs out of her own moment of astonishment. 'Stop clapping!' she said brusquely. 'None of this is for your entertainment, Immi. This is serious.'

'You could have fooled me,' said the librarian cheerfully. 'C'mon, lighten up a bit.'

'Lighten up!' Anaïs threw her hands in the air. 'Don't you know what's going on out there?'

'Sort of.' Immi hunched her shoulders. 'Not my problem.'

'What? How is it not your problem?'

Immi shrugged. 'It's not my job.'

'But—'

Ella interjected. Stepping between the two women, she called for calm.

Anaïs simmered. 'Fine,' she said quietly, realising that it was pointless to argue with the librarian.

'What did it say?' enquired the Apothecary, cocking her head at Sappho.

Anaïs stared at the ladybird's soft eyes. 'The same as before, Ella. We need to find my mother.'

DEUS AND IGNATIUS

In downtown Catania, the Ethnarch stood among the rubble. He was clearly feeling out of sorts. A fresh wound etched a bloody line down his left cheek. Scorch marks ran around the circumference of his bare skull like a headband.

Iggy studied the scarring. 'What happened to you?'

'Don't ask,' said Deus. 'It will heal.'

'You better hope so. It looks terrible.'

'Thanks for your concern.'

'I was just being courteous.' Iggy sneered. 'To be perfectly honest, considering what I know now, I don't give a damn about you.'

Deus frowned. He winced as his taut skin pulled at the wound on his face.

The Inquisitor puffed his cheeks. He loudly expelled the air they contained. 'Why didn't you tell me the shade was Nan?'

Deus pursed his lips. 'You wouldn't have cooperated.'

'You don't know that,' said Iggy.

'Believe me, I do,' retorted Deus gruffly.

Tilting his head forward, the Inquisitor fell silent. Simmering, he glanced up at his father's face from under his eyebrows.

'What's your mother doing?' enquired Deus.

Ignatius straightened. He breathed deeply through his nostrils. He nodded with his chin towards the peak of Mount Etna above them. 'I guess she's still mopping up the volcano.'

Deus glanced up at the mountain towering above them. To one side a sizeable chunk of the crater had broken off, creating a massive landslide. Several lines of lava ran horizontally around its slopes. The flow of lava towards the base of the mountain appeared to have halted. However, it was apparent more was on its way. An explosion of rock flew skywards from the crater. The Ethnarch flinched.

In anticipation of the fallout, both men hurried under the awning of a nearby building. Apart from its facade and the rickety canvas frame attached to it, the rest of the structure had collapsed.

'Your mother shouldn't be doing that,' said Deus. 'It's your job.'

'Help arrived from the Organisation. She told me to go.'

Deus shrugged. He grunted and massaged the base of his spine. He arched his top lip. 'Her choice. It suits her, anyway. She was only ever good enough to be a cleaner.' He flicked the small stones from a large block of masonry and sat on it.

Ignatius flared his nostrils at the comment about his mother. It took all his self-control to prevent him spitting in his father's face. The snide expression on it made him sick. He cleared his throat. 'And now?'

'The girl has to be stopped.'

'I thought you were doing that?'

'I am.' Deus maintained a straight face, belying the truth about his defeat and hiding the fact he had confronted Anaïs and then failed to capture her. 'I need time to consider how we should deal with her.' He removed a handkerchief from his coat pocket and dabbed his cheek with it. Dropping his hand, he examined the bloodied cloth.

Iggy cast a close eye over the Ethnarch's cheek. 'You should get someone to have a look at that.'

'I said it will be fine,' replied Deus, seemingly unfazed by his injury. 'As you have nothing to do now, perhaps you can help me.'

Iggy sniffed. 'Right now, I'm in no mood to do anything for you.'

'Why? What's the problem.'

'Haven't you listened to anything I've said?' Iggy snarled through his teeth. 'The problem is my sister.'

Deus sighed. 'Will you drop that already? She was never in any real danger.'

'That's not how I see it,' muttered the Inquisitor.

Deus discarded his comment with a wave of his hand. 'It's of no importance what you think, Ignatius. You know about her now. That should be enough. I have no wish to discuss her further. We have more important things to do.' He cast a rueful eye over the ruins surrounding them.

The Inquisitor opened his mouth to interject.

The Ethnarch cut him off. 'I will convene with the Brotherhood and we will devise a plan.' He studied his son's face. 'Against my better judgement—considering how you have continually failed—see if you can make amends and find Anaïs. But don't approach her until we have made a decision.'

Ignatius studied his father's eyes, trying to read them. Something in them made him mistrust his true intentions. He decided to conceal his feelings. *We'll see about that.* He mimicked Deus's deadpan expression and nodded silently.

'You should be happy with that arrangement,' said the Ethnarch. 'That way you get to keep an eye on your sister as well.'

Iggy's face soured. A hailstorm of rocks prevented him responding further. They peppered the canvas roof above them, causing both men to duck instinctively. The awning swayed on its feeble supports.

Deus yelled above the cacophony, 'Do as I say, Ignatius!'

As the awning succumbed to the weight of rocks, the two men rushed out from under it in opposite directions. Going their separate ways, they both sought temporary refuge as the city of Catania laboured under the destructive force of Mount Etna. One of the men felt more turmoil than even a volcano could supply.

ADRIFT

A sudden sideways shunt slowed the Catamarine considerably. A whooping siren sounded in the wheelhouse. It was deafening. Ella clapped her hands over her ears. Anaïs did the same.

'What's going on?' Anaïs screamed over the cacophony.

Ella gestured wildly with her elbows. She mouthed the words, 'I don't know.'

The Catamarine lurched to one side. Ella and Anaïs released their ears and grabbed the console for support. Every single light on it flashed incessantly. The whooping continued unabated.

Across the cabin Immi was less fortunate.

Caught off balance and failing to find anything solid to grab hold of, she was thrown violently across the cabin. Crashing against a bulkhead, her forehead took the full brunt of the impact. It smashed into the rounded underside of a storage compartment secured to the ceiling and jutting out from the wall. Her perfectly arranged hairdo thrown in disarray, she slumped to the floor.

The Catamarine continued to buck and roll like a bronco. The librarian's limp body followed its movement, sliding backwards and forwards across the floor. Not daring to release her grip on the console, Anaïs watched helplessly as Immi accumulated more bruises.

Ella punched a button on the console. The whooping ceased as quickly as it had begun.

The ringing in the witch's ears persisted. Anaïs flexed her jaw and watched Ella do the same. The ringing in her head subsided. She stuck her fingers in her ears and wiggled them. 'What happened?'

'No idea,' said the Apothecary. 'It felt like we hit something, or something hit us.'

'And now?'

'Something seems to be interfering with our guidance systems.' Ella's eyes roved over the console. 'We're rudderless. We don't have any control. We're going to have to surface and have a look.'

'Can we even do that?'

'I hope so,' said Ella grimly. 'We're being tossed around like a cork. We'll have to fix it otherwise we'll be in real trouble.'

A sudden surge of current pushed the vessel sideways, causing the two women to grasp the console even more securely for support. Still on the console, Sappho scuttled up Anaïs's arm and affixed herself to the witch's shoulder.

The reassuring presence of the ladybird gave Anaïs the confidence she needed to proceed. 'Punch it, Ella!' she cried. 'Let's get to the surface!'

'Right you are!' exclaimed the Apothecary. She hit the green button with the upwards arrow. An explosion of air bubbles outside blocked their view through the wheelhouse's windows.

Anaïs stared at them. It was as if they were floating in a bottle of carbonated water. Although her view was totally obscured, she sensed the vessel rise. She breathed a tentative sigh of relief. 'Thank goodness that still works.'

Ella nodded in agreement. 'Yes, thank goodness.'

Within moments the Catamarine broke the surface and stabilised. Sunlight streamed into the wheelhouse. Anaïs and Ella shielded their eyes against the piercing rays. Once their vision had adjusted they were presented with a vast emptiness. Surrounding them was open water with no landfall in sight.

'That's not good,' said Ella.

'No, it's not,' replied Anaïs. 'But we have to do something.' She glanced down at Immi's crumpled body. 'First, let's get her comfortable. Then perhaps you can look if there's any kind of readout which might show damage. I can go look on the deck.'

Ella nodded. 'Okay.'

Together they laid Immi out flat on the floor. They checked for broken bones. Mercifully, they found none. Kneeling next to her, Anaïs studied the librarian's face with concern. Her forehead was swollen and a dark bruise had already begun to form. 'That's one hell of bump.'

'It certainly is,' said Ella. 'She's going to wake up with one serious headache.'

'Yep. Let's hope there's no permanent damage. Maybe, once we've sorted this out, I can scan her body with the promptuary to check.'

'At least she's quiet.'

'You're right there.' Anaïs grinned. 'That's a little miracle in itself.' She stood, collected her handbook, slipped it in her coat pocket and walked to the door. 'I'll go have a look outside.'

'Okay,' said Ella. 'Let me know if you find something.' She cocked her head at the console. 'I'll see what I can find here.'

Anaïs nodded. She unlatched the door. She had to put her entire weight against it to break the rubber seals. They separated with a loud ripping sound. The door flew open and she practically toppled out onto the deck. Regaining her balance, she stepped outside. She shimmied around the wheelhouse and inspected the bow of the vessel. Finding nothing she proceeded towards the stern. The raised deck did not permit her to get to the rear end of the vessel. She leaned over the railing and peered over the edge. Below her the pristine waters were clear. She could make out the aft of the Catamarine submerged under a metre of water. A large, unidentifiable black mass covered the stern. Anaïs scratched her head. *Is that a net or seaweed?*

She turned and called out to the Apothecary. 'Ella, I think I've found the problem.'

Ella stuck her head out the door. 'What is it?'

'Something is wrapped around the stern,' said Anaïs. 'I'm not exactly sure what it is, but I think if we can free it we can get moving again. Hopefully there's no other damage.'

'How do you want to do that?'

'No idea.' Anaïs twisted her lips. 'We have to get down there, though. Can you swim?'

Ella cleared her throat. 'Ahem, no.'

Anaïs raised an eyebrow. 'You can't swim?'

'No, never took the time to learn.'

'But you're on a boat. Doesn't that bother you.'

Ella shrugged. 'Nope, not really. There are life vests. Can you swim?'

'Yes, but I don't think I'll be strong enough to free it.'

'What do you want to do then?'

Anaïs hunched her shoulders. 'Dunno.'

The sudden movement brought the ladybird into action. Attached to Anaïs's back, Sappho slid her front legs over the witch's shoulders. She crossed them over Anaïs's chest. Under Anaïs's arms, she did the same with her middle legs. Grabbing hold of her front legs with her middle legs she created a sort of harness. She slid her hind legs around Anaïs's waist and locked them onto one another. The whole arrangement was tight and snug but gave Anaïs freedom to breathe.

Slightly taken aback, Anaïs spoke to the insect. 'Sappho? What are you doing?'

The ladybird peeled open her elytra and unfurled her wings. A gust of wind caught them. Taken by surprise, the force sent Anaïs stumbling backwards. She almost tumbled over the handrail running around the deck. She grabbed the railing for support, wrapping her arms around it to prevent herself from being carried away by the wind.

'Anaïs!' cried Ella.

'I'm okay,' said the witch through gritted teeth, fighting another gust of wind. It took all her strength to avoid being swept over the side. 'I think.'

Ella eyed the ladybird's enormous wings. 'We have a solution.'

'What?'

The Apothecary grinned. 'You can fly.'

LADYBIRDS

I must apologise, but I feel the need to explain some things about the humble ladybird.

'Oh, no,' you say, 'not another science lesson.'

There's nothing to fear. Everything I say has a purpose. So, at the risk of causing your eyes to glaze over, let's do this.

Ladybirds, or lady beetles, or Coccinellidae, or whatever you want to call them, are a freak of nature. Whereas many insects never make a complete metamorphosis, they do.

They have four cycles in their life. They don't hatch out of a cocoon. It all starts with a cluster of eggs. Once out of an egg they do their thing fully exposed on a leaf. They make a magical transformation. Firstly they go from larvae, a sort of hairy slug, to pupae, closely resembling the finished product. From there they metamorphose into a completely different form. Finally, the spotted elytra—which is a protective shell concealing their wings—

reconfigures itself into a different shape and colour pattern.

Pretty amazing if you think about it. Not that different to the stages that a certain little witch has been going through. Exposed to the outside world, Anaïs has also made astonishing jumps in physical development.

There are a phenomenal number of species of these wonderful creatures. All with different bodies, spots and colourings. Something like 6,000 at last count. It's safe to say the world is infested with all manner of ladybirds. However, it should be noted, there is only one Sappho.

Traditional views of witches usually bestow on them a familiar. This is yet another fallacy created by naturals. Witches don't have the time to take care of an animal. Having one will only hamper their freedom of movement.

Take, for instance, the activity of temporarily taking over the body of a natural. Possession of a host takes an enormous amount of concentration. You can't go around jumping into someone else's body and be stuck worrying about whether you remembered to feed your cat. Not to mention the constant practice of globetrotting. Alone, a witch can sneak through all kinds of border controls. Having to do that with a familiar would make the process all the more complicated.

In the community there has been talk of only one other witch who had a familiar. Supposedly it was an elephant. This must have been highly impractical, to say the least. It's not exactly something you can smuggle on board a flight in your carry-on luggage.

Therefore, it is somewhat of an anomaly that Anaïs

has come into the possession of one. Clearly her tasks require more assistance than an ordinary witch. Lilith, with all her knowledge, is certainly aware of this. Otherwise she would not have bestowed on Anaïs such a special gift.

The fact Sappho has extensive experience with metamorphosis would also give Anaïs a true confidante through her journey. Not only that, it is fast becoming clear she is more magical than merely serving as a conduit for communication.

REPAIRS

Anaïs looked down at the rope in her hands. 'You think this will work?'

'We can only try,' said Ella.

Anaïs flicked her head over her shoulder at the ladybird on her back. 'But what if she decides to put her wings away.'

'Tell her not to do that. You can talk to her can't you?'

Anaïs nodded.

'Then do that,' said Ella. 'Here.' She indicated the rope. 'Give me that. I'll tie it around you. That way you'll have your arms free and I won't lose you.'

'So, I'm going to be a kite now?'

Ella smiled. 'Yes.'

'Great!' Anaïs rolled her eyes. She handed the rope to Ella and watched with some trepidation as the Apothecary tied it around her waist. 'And when I'm up there, what am I going to do?'

'You'll think of something.'

Anaïs frowned. She sighed and shoved her hand in her coat pocket. Her knuckles jarred on a hard object. 'Ow!' She wrapped her fingers around the object. Anaïs's eyes widened. 'That's it!'

'What's it?'

'This.' Anaïs pulled the object out of her pocket. She opened her palm to reveal Marilyn's compact. 'I can try this. I'm not sure if it will work, but if it's powerful enough to fry hellhounds, then it should be able to do the same with whatever's jamming things up back there.'

'Okay,' murmured Ella through tight lips. 'But don't go setting us on fire.'

'I'll try not to.'

'Okay,' said Ella, stepping back to admire her handiwork. 'I think you're secure. Just a second, one more thing.' She took the end of the rope, knelt and tied it to the railing. She stood. 'You ready?'

'Ready as I'll ever be,' said Anaïs with uncertainty.

Ella gave her a reassuring smile. 'Good. Don't worry. You'll do fine.'

Anaïs closed her eyes. *This is madness.* She sent out her thoughts. '*Lilith, are you there?*'

To Anaïs's relief her grandmother responded immediately. *'Yes.'*

'Excellent!' She grinned. *'I need a little physical help from Sappho. Is that possible?'*

'Of course, just ask her.'

'Thanks.'

'Always here to help, Anaïs. I said it before: you have all the tools you need. Trust them.'

Anaïs breathed deeply and exhaled. She opened her eyes. 'Ella, take the rope. Let's do this.'

The Apothecary nodded. She inched backwards along the deck towards the wheelhouse, slowly paying out the rope.

'Sappho? Let's fly,' said Anaïs.

The ladybird flexed her wings and shook them. A cloud of purple dust swirled around the witch. Sappho stretched her wings full-length. A gust of wind caught them. It lifted Anaïs off the deck. She caught her breath.

Sappho flapped her wings in one great sweep and they soared into the air. Anaïs choked. Then spluttered. She sucked in a mouthful of air, forcing her lungs to expand. With her heart in her throat she tried to regulate her breathing. Then she began to giggle uncontrollably. She cleared her throat and attempted to pull herself together.

'Wow!' she exclaimed. She looked down. The boat appeared tiny—a speck in the ocean below her—Ella a miniature figure standing on the deck.

The Apothecary had released the rope, her palms burnt by the speed with which Sappho had taken off. Grimacing, she shook her hands. Cupping her palms she cooled them with her breath.

'Sorry, Ella!' yelled Anaïs.

Ella tilted her head to the sky. 'Are you okay?' she yelled back.

Anaïs glanced around her. Her position stable with Sappho floating on the updrafts, she nodded enthusiastically. She turned her head to the side. 'Sappho, can you get me down to the rear of the boat.'

The ladybird dipped her wings. They dropped as suddenly as they had risen, plummeting down towards the Catamarine. Anaïs yelped, again forced to catch her breath. Sappho stopped their descent a few metres above and astern of the vessel.

Anaïs let out a puff of air. 'Sappho! I'm not used to this. Take it easy, will you?' She waited for her heartbeat to slow before squinting to appraise the damage to the Catamarine. The waters were so pristine she could see the rudder jutting out from the rear of the vessel. Upon closer inspection she found that wrapped around it was a fishing net. The net, full of plastic and other refuse, was a twisted mess.

Anaïs flipped open the compact. Catching the sun's rays, she directed it towards the netting. A thin beam of hot yellow light pierced the water. It hit the edge of the netting. Guiding the beam across the thickest part of it and avoiding the rudder, she severed it in half. The two sections floated free.

Anaïs snapped the compact shut and punched the sky. 'Yes!'

A whooping of the siren from the wheelhouse drew her attention. On deck, Ella gesticulated wildly. At first Anaïs thought she was celebrating with her. Upon seeing the fear in her eyes, she realised this was not the case.

'What!' cried Anaïs.

The Apothecary was yelling but her words were obscured, carried away by the wind rushing around Anaïs's ears. She waved her hands next to them, indicating to Ella that she could not hear her.

To Anaïs's horror the water around the vessel began

to churn. It started to flow over the deck. The Catamarine began to submerge. Ella about-faced and swished through the water to the wheelhouse door. She stepped inside. She leaned out through the doorway. Her face flushed, she jabbed her finger repeatedly at something behind the little witch. Anaïs tried to look over her shoulder but her view was blocked by Sappho's wings.

On deck the water began to lap over the lip of the doorway. In panic, Ella threw her hands in the air and clasped her head. Anaïs waved to her. She indicated that Ella should close the door. The Apothecary shook her head emphatically. Anaïs returned by gesturing as she had before. Although deep down she sensed it would not be the case, she gave Ella a thumbs-up and tried to communicate with her facial expression that all would be fine.

Ella relented. The last Anaïs saw of her as she closed the door was a pained look of helplessness on her face.

The vessel continue to sink until all Anaïs could see was the roof of the wheelhouse. It too began to fade from view as the Catamarine submerged into water so deep the sun could not penetrate. Anaïs felt a tug at her waist. She began to descend. With the rope still connecting her to the vessel, they were being dragged down with it.

'Oh no!' she shrieked.

She panicked. Frantically she wrenched at the knot Ella had fastened. Under tension it would not budge.

'No, no, no!'

The rope pulled her steadily closer to the peaks of

the waves beneath her. She could almost touch them with her toes.

She mentally slapped herself. *Pull yourself together!*

Breathing deeply to calm herself, she sucked sea air in through her nostrils. Its salty tang cleared her head. It brought her focus. Lilith's reassuring words of advice flooded her mind. She could do it. She had all the tools she needed.

She turned her hand over and opened her palm. Dumbstruck, she stared at Marilyn's compact lying in it. *All the tools I need.* She flipped it open with her thumb and directed its mirror towards the sun. The reflected beam it produced cut a line towards the distant horizon. She angled the compact, guiding its beam down across the rope. The fibres began to smoke, then caught fire. The rope snapped.

Released from its grip, Anaïs and Sappho shot upwards. Gusts of wind spun them in an out-of-control spiral. Spinning around and around, Anaïs lost all sense of direction. She screamed the ladybird's name. Her new accomplice did not let her down.

Sappho set her wings taut, stabilising them. They came to a halt high above the ocean, bobbing on the updrafts and facing the direction Ella had previously indicated.

The blood drained from Anaïs's face. She gasped. Bearing down of them was a gigantic wave. The peak of it towered above them. Its height and appearance were not unlike the snow-tipped slopes of Mount Etna.

The panic Anaïs had managed to subdue moments earlier returned with ferocity.

THE CREST

With her eyes fixed on the oncoming wave, Anaïs fought to eliminate her panic. She dropped the compact into her pocket. She rubbed her face vigorously. She slapped her cheeks. She growled. She clenched her fists.

'Snap out of it!' she yelled at herself. 'You've faced bigger things than this!' She glanced at the wave. 'Well, maybe not. But anyway!'

Reassuring herself worked. Her initial panic subsided. She puffed her cheeks and breathed easily.

'Sappho!' she called over her shoulder to the ladybird. 'Get us higher!'

Sappho responded at once, furiously beating her wings. The sound of them displacing air was tremendous. It buffeted Anaïs's ears. Gradually they gained elevation. Anaïs felt the air chill and become thin. She pulled her coat tightly around herself and measured her breath.

The wave continued to approach, closing in on them at a rapid pace.

'Sappho, get us over it!'

The ladybird obliged. Continuing to climb, she banked to the right and set a course along the face of the wave. It was a sight to behold. Anaïs tempered her fear and took in the wave's magnificence for a split second. Although terrifying in its gigantic proportions, somehow it was all at once awe-inspiring, breathtaking and beautiful—nature in all its fury. Its crest, capped by a solid, thick, white line, sent spray flying tens of metres into the air.

Sappho beat her wings harder. With each beat they gained altitude. Anaïs watched the wave nearing. She bit her lip and willed Sappho on. With no possibility of outrunning it, all they could do was go higher.

They pulled level with the crest. Anaïs saw peaks within peaks. It was more like a mountain range than a wave—terrifyingly, a virtually unstoppable mountain on the move. Spray from the crest rained down on them, saturating Anaïs. Catching an updraft, Sappho changed direction, angling them towards the cloud of spray.

The ladybird flapped her wings once and folded them flat to her side. They shot forward with such momentum it was as if they were being launched from a cannon. Instinctively Anaïs locked her forearms in front of her face. She hugged her own skull. They ploughed through the cloud of spray. Anaïs peered between her arms but could no longer see. Water slapped her face. She made slivers of her eyes. She licked her lips and spat, screwing up her face at the salty taste.

What had begun as a fine mist became large droplets. They stung as they hit the bare skin on the backs of her hands. She lowered her head, setting her chin on her chest, shielding it as best she could with her arms. She blinked water free from her eyelashes and stared at the crooks of her elbows. Water ran down the inside of her collar. She shivered as it trickled down the inner surface of her clothing, an icy rivulet running along the naked flesh on her spine.

Although virtually blind, she could still hear. The roar from the wave was indescribable. A continuous roll of thunder. The noise ebbed and flowed slightly, yet pounded her ears unabated. It was deafening. Almost as if she were within the swell and not soaring above it.

Feeling helpless, with no other option, Anaïs succumbed to the situation. She let herself go. She put all her trust in the ladybird.

'Sappho, you can do this!' she yelled.

Confirming the trust bestowed on her, Sappho flicked her wingtips. Surging forward, their velocity increased. The rain on Anaïs's hands struck harder, now feeling like hailstones. She grimaced. She fought the pain.

She opened her mouth and screamed at the top of her lungs. More than anything it was a cry of defiance. Water filled her mouth. It ran out of the corners and down over her chin. She spluttered.

Then.

In an instant.

As it had begun.

It all stopped.

Suddenly, there was no rain—no water—only crisp air drying her skin.

She dropped her arms. Sunshine hit her face. She closed her eyes, tilted her head back and basked in its warmth.

They were through.

FREEFALL

Anaïs wiped the water from her face as best she could. The sleeve of her wet coat only made it worse. She gave up and let the wind from the speed of their flight dry her. Squinting in the sunlight, she looked below her. She gulped. They were very high. Scarily high. However, they did seem to be losing altitude.

Far below her was open water. A vast blue slate. She lifted her head and looked into the distance. Thankfully, they were fast approaching land.

Directly before them she saw a massive city ringed on three sides by mountains. The peaks on the range in the far distance were snow-capped. The city itself seemed covered in snow as well. Everything was white. Anaïs peered at it. They were losing altitude fast. Gradually, she could make out more detail. Snow was not covering the city. The buildings themselves were white.

'Sappho,' she called over shoulder. 'We have to land.'

Anaïs looked down along her body to her feet. The ladybird's wings were wrapped around her legs.

'Sappho? Did you hear me?'

The ladybird responded by attempting to shake her wings. They flapped uselessly against Anaïs's legs.

Anaïs frowned. *What's going on?* She scrutinised the ladybird's wings closely. They were soaked, glistening with droplets of water. *Oh, no! Her wings are too wet. She can't use them.*

Anaïs turned her attention to their flight trajectory. They were now falling at an uncomfortable rate. The wind on her face stretched her skin taut. Tears gathered in her eyes and obscured her view. She snatched the beret from her head and rummaged inside. Finding Elvis's sunglasses, she slipped them on. Her vision cleared. She replaced the beret, pulling it low over her ears. She glanced back at their trajectory.

They had reached the coastline and were now heading directly towards the centre of the city. Anaïs watched the buildings pass beneath her. The city was incredibly congested. Except for small gaps created by the narrow streets, the buildings were solidly packed against one another. Panic returned, producing a knot in her throat.

Where are we going to land in all of this?

She pleaded with the ladybird, 'Sappho? Please try again?'

Anaïs glanced down at the wings. Sappho was doing her utmost. She had let her wings go limp. The wind caught them. They unfurled. Fluttering in the stiff breeze created by their descent, they began to dry.

Will they dry fast enough?

Anaïs redirected her focus to their flight path. Now only a couple of hundred metres above the ground, she scanned the city for a soft landing site. To her left was an ancient ruin perched on a solitary hill. She recognised it immediately: the Acropolis.

We're in Athens.

On top of the hill, the Parthenon and the plateau surrounding it were filled with tourists.

Too busy.

Beyond the Acropolis and before her lay an open area. Although littered with large blocks of masonry, there were still enough spaces in which to land.

The Temple of Zeus. That could work. She soon discounted the option. *Too exposed.*

Beyond it were large swathes of green.

That's it. One of those parks. We'll be hidden. The trees will break our fall. Maybe.

She stretched out her arm and jabbed with her finger, pointing towards the parks. 'Sappho, there.'

Using her elytra Sappho adjusted their flight path. They arced towards the trees. Anaïs covered her face with her arms. She pulled up her knees and curled into a ball, steeling herself for impact.

In the final moments, only metres above the tree tops, Sappho gained control over her wings. She snapped them out full span. In their rigid state, she turned them to catch the wind. It slowed their flight considerably. However, not enough to stall. With a swish of her wings, she flipped them over, spinning Anaïs and herself a half-turn around their axis. Now flying backwards, with Anaïs on top of her, Sappho folded her wings in, cocooning the little witch.

They hit the trees.

In a ball, with her face still covered, Anaïs was unaware of what Sappho had done. She heard the snapping of twigs and branches. Also an almighty crash as they hit the ground. Confusion reigned. Why could she not feel the full brunt of the impact?

Then they were momentarily airborne. Again the movement stopped as they connected with something solid. This process repeated itself several times. Each time, in between, they floated seemingly in nothingness. It felt as though she was encased in a bouncing rubber ball.

After what felt like minutes, but were in fact only seconds, they came to a final halt. Sappho released the witch. Anaïs rolled out of her cocoon. She stretched her legs and lay flat on her back. She stared at the clear sky above her and breathed out a tentative sigh of relief.

Unbelievable! I'm alive.

She checked her body, running her hands down over her torso to her thighs. *No damage.* She rolled onto her stomach. She got up on all fours, stood and dusted off her knees. She cast her eyes on her surroundings. She was on a slab of rock in a small clearing. Nearby, Sappho lay motionless on her side.

Anaïs covered her mouth in alarm. 'Oh, no! Sappho!'

She rushed across to the ladybird. Kneeling beside

her Anaïs turned Sappho over onto her abdomen. Anaïs stared at the four large black spots on her elytra. A yellow substance oozed from a long slash cutting into the surface of one of them.

'Sappho? Are you bleeding?'

First there was no reaction. Then the spots slowly configured themselves into a mournful face.

Anaïs was beside herself. 'Sappho, why did you do that? It wasn't necessary.'

The eyelids on the face batted at her.

'Lilith? Are you there?'

The voice of her grandmother permeated Anaïs's head. *'Yes, Anaïs.'*

'Will she be all right?'

'Yes, Anaïs,' said Lilith. *'There is no permanent damage. But you will have to care for her until she recovers.'*

'How?'

'I told you. You have all the tools you need.'

Frustrated and irritated that her grandmother continued to be so elusive, Anaïs sighed. She considered Lilith's words for a moment.

'Again with the tools!' she grumbled.

She took off her beret and shoved her hand into it. *Tools. Tools. What tools?* She closed her eyes and concentrated. *What do I have to repair ladybirds with?*

A small, slender object jumped into her hand. She pulled it out.

Grinning at what lay in her open palm, she murmured, 'Thank goodness for apothecaries.'

CROWD CONTROL

Anaïs unscrewed the cap of the silver tube Ella had given to her on Malta. Then, she had used the salve to heal her burnt hand. She eyed the vicious wound on the ladybird's elytra. Mentally, she crossed her fingers.

'I hope this works on other injuries.'

She squeezed a glob of the milky liquid onto her fingertips. Gently, she applied it to the damaged area on Sappho's elytra. The eyes in the face on the ladybird's back widened. A broad grin spread across it. The yellow discharge dissipated and the slash across the face sealed itself. Miraculously, it began to disappear.

'Ha!' cried Anaïs, punching the air in jubilation. 'It works!' She replaced the cap on the tube and dropped it into her beret, along with her sunglasses. She flipped the hat onto her head.

Sappho stood. She flexed her legs and elytra. Her wings, which had dried, fanned out beside her like a cape. Opening her elytra fully, she folded her wings under their protective casing and closed them.

Anaïs climbed to her feet. With a cock of her head and wave of her finger she beckoned the ladybird to her. Sappho scooted up Anaïs's leg and climbed around onto her back.

Anaïs took a deep breath and exhaled. 'Right! Let's get out of here.'

With a renewed sense of purpose she strode across the rocky slab. She jumped down off its edge onto a well-worn path. Following it through the trees, she reached a high fence. The path led her along it until she came across a small gateway.

Anaïs stopped. She tried to get her bearings. Looking up through the trees to her left she saw the Acropolis in the distance. She opened the gate and stepped through it. On the footpath outside she found herself caught in a throng of people. Swept up in the crush of their bodies, she had no option but to go with their flow. They were all moving in one direction, taking her away from the Acropolis.

She fought to stay on her feet. *What's going on now?*

Behind her, in the direction from which the crowd was coming, she heard loud voices. The sound of men yelling out crackled orders through megaphones. The throng thickened further. Within moments the crowd slowed and came to a complete standstill.

Sandwiched between a woman in her early twenties and a swarthy-looking middle-aged man, Anaïs lifted her elbows to create a bit of space for herself. She inadvertently nudged the woman in the ribs. She shot Anaïs a look of intense irritation.

'Sorry,' said Anaïs apologetically.

The woman's glare softened.

'Er,' ventured Anaïs tentatively. 'Do you speak English?'

The woman nodded.

'Could you tell me what's going on?'

The woman eyed Anaïs quizzically. 'You don't know what's happening?'

Anaïs shook her head.

'The government is rounding people up,' said the woman. 'I can't understand why you wouldn't know that. It's been going on all morning.'

'I just arrived here.' Anaïs cast her thoughts back to the crash landing. *Please don't ask me how I arrived.*

The woman assessed the little witch. 'Where are your parents?'

That's an excellent question. Anaïs grinned to herself. *I wish I knew the answer to that one. It would solve a heap of problems.* She cleared her throat. 'We got separated.'

'Oh,' said the woman with concern. 'That's terrible. You better stick with me then.'

'Thank you for your kindness,' said Anaïs.

'Oh, it's no bother. We're all stuck in this together. We should help each other.'

'Stuck in what together?' A sudden sense of foreboding caused Anaïs to furrow her brow. 'Why are people being rounded up?'

'To check everyone,' said the woman.

'Check them for what?'

'To see if they are alive.'

'Alive?'

'Yes.' The woman frowned. 'Where have you been? Haven't you seen the news? It's happening everywhere.'

Everywhere? Anaïs tried to contain her apprehension and keep a straight face. She shrugged as nonchalantly as she could. 'I don't watch the news. My parents think it's bad for me.'

'Mmm,' said the woman. 'They might have something there.'

Furtively, Anaïs glanced around her. She peered through the gaps between the bodies in front of her. A few metres away one person caught her attention: an elderly woman swaying lethargically on the spot. For a moment her appearance flickered and changed. It revealed a boy not much older than Anaïs's physical age. The change occurred in a split-second, the camouflage immediately reasserting itself. Anaïs checked those standing next to him. No one seemed to have noticed the transformation. She sucked in her breath. *Shades. They're rounding up shades.*

'Like I said, it's happening everywhere,' said the woman.

'Everywhere? What's happening everywhere?'

'This. Checking people. All around the world. I don't believe any of it, mind you.' She crossed herself. 'But better to be safe than sorry, I suppose.'

'How can they do that?'

'Who?'

'The government,' said Anaïs.

'Emergency protocol.'

Anaïs frowned. 'It doesn't seem right to me.'

The woman hunched her shoulders. 'Me either, but what are you going to do?'

'Elect another government?'

The woman laughed. 'Fat chance that will make a difference. They're all the same.'

The crowd surged forward a few steps. In the crush Anaïs was lifted off her feet and carried along with them. She tried vainly to stay grounded, but could only brush the footpath with the tips of her toes. Once the movement stopped, the crush eased. She dropped back to the ground. She wiped her brow with her sleeve. *This sucks big time! I've got to get out of here.*

'Nice backpack,' said the woman, attempting to make small talk and seemingly oblivious to the witch's predicament.

'Sorry?'

'Your backpack,' said the woman, eyeing Sappho. 'The ladybird. Where'd you get it?'

Anaïs turned her body to prevent the woman from closely examining Sappho. 'On one of the islands.'

'Gonna have to get me one of those.'

'I'm afraid it's one of a kind,' murmured Anaïs. *Now I've really got to get out of here.*

'Pity,' said the woman, mildly disappointed.

The crowd surged forward again. This time Anaïs was more prepared and managed to stay on her feet. To her relief a crowd barrier appeared in the throng, separating her from the woman. Anaïs pushed against the people beside her to put some distance between them. *Sorry, lady. You ask too many questions.*

The woman tried to force her way back to the witch without success. She threw her hands up in frustration. She yelled at Anaïs, 'Will you be all right?'

'Yes!' Anaïs called back. 'I'll be fine.'

'See you on the other side then,' she replied cheerfully.

'Yep,' said Anaïs. 'See you on the other side.' She ducked and slipped between the legs of two large men to get out of sight. *No offence, lady, but there's no way I want to see you on the other side.*

The crowd stopped moving. Anaïs wiggled into a standing position. She glanced between the gaps around her, trying to spot more shades. There did not seem to be any.

The surge forward resumed. Taken off guard, Anaïs was once again lifted off her feet. She decided to take advantage of it. Using the shoulders of the people beside her, she pulled herself higher to get a better view. For a moment she caught a glimpse of where the crowd was heading.

Before them was the horseshoe shape of a huge, ancient amphitheatre. Constructed entirely of white marble, the tiers of seating encompassing the central arena reflected the winter sunlight. There were hundreds of people milling at ground level. From her viewpoint, only the lower seats seemed to be occupied. A line of uniformed men stood before her in the open end of the horseshoe.

As the crowd continued forward the pressure of the bodies around her ebbed. She dropped back to the ground as the throng thinned.

Finally! A bit of room!

Spying a gap she could squeeze through, she took a step forward to rush through it. A man stepped into her path, barring her way. She tried to dodge him, but he moved sideways to block her path. He grabbed her by the shoulders, his grip so fierce he dug his thumb-tips into her collarbone.

'Ow!' she cried.

She tried to shake him loose. He held his stance. Anaïs swore. *Security guards are a pain in the butt!* With her face flushed with exasperation, she looked up at his.

Oh, no!

She sighed heavily, gritted her teeth and snarled to herself. *Great! Just what I need right now!*

FRIEND OR FOE

The Inquisitor relaxed his grip on her shoulders. 'Sorry, I didn't mean to hurt you.'

What? Sorry?

'I just didn't want you running away.'

Of course you didn't. You never do, you wacko!

He spoke softly, his eyes filled with concern. 'Are you okay?'

Am I okay? Anaïs forced her eyes shut. She blinked to clear her disorientated mind. *What the heck?*

He continued, his voice uncharacteristically soothing. 'We need to get out of here, Anaïs.'

We? Confused by his attitude, she knotted her brow and shook her head. 'I'm not going anywhere with you.'

'Don't be like that,' he pleaded, practically begging her. 'I'm trying to help you.'

'Help me!' She flared her nostrils. 'Since when have you ever helped me!'

'I know, I know. You're right,' he conceded. 'The

situation has changed, though. I can explain. Just not here. Please believe me.'

She glanced around, desperately searching for an escape route. Hemmed in by the crowd, there was none. 'Believe you? Why should I believe you?'

'I don't know what I can say to convince you. You'll just have to trust me.'

'Trust?' She snorted. 'That's something you have to earn.'

'I know.' He looked down at his hands on her shoulders. Realising the grip he still had on her, he released her. Raising his hands he held them palms out next to his face, as if he were succumbing to an armed robber. 'Look, you're free to go if you want. I won't stop you.'

Anaïs raised an eyebrow.

He dropped his arms. His eyes darted around, scrutinising the throng of people. He returned his focus to the little witch's face, fixing her with a serious stare. 'Anaïs, you may not want it, but you will need my help.'

Anaïs sneered at him. 'Give me one good reason why I should go with you.'

'You're not safe here,' he said. 'Neither of us is safe here. I'm taking a huge risk as it is.'

'Risk?'

'Several risks, actually,' he mused. 'But, right now, there's a particularly immediate one.' He flicked his thumb over his shoulder at the amphitheatre behind him. 'We have to get out of here before we end up in there.'

'What's in there?'

'Shades. Hundreds of them.'

She cocked her head to one side. 'Why is that such a problem? I'm used to dealing with shades.'

'Not like this.'

'I'll cope.'

He shook his head vigorously. 'No, you won't.'

'Why?'

'At the moment the shades themselves are not the main problem.'

Anaïs frowned. 'What is then?'

'The fact they will reveal who we are.'

'Oh.' Anaïs bit her bottom lip.

'Yes,' said Iggy, satisfied that she understood the gravity of their predicament.

During their conversation the crowd had ignored the two of them. People had filed past them in an orderly manner. Now the crowd thickened. A shove in her back sent Anaïs careening into the Inquisitor's arms. He planted his boots in an effort to hold their position. The momentum of the throng was too great.

Grabbing Anaïs by the shoulders with one arm, the Inquisitor bent down and slipped his other arm under the backs of her knees. He stood, sweeping her up into his arms.

'Stop!' she protested, trying to scramble out of his embrace. 'What the heck are you doing?'

He ignored her pleas and held her firm. Using Anaïs's trailing legs like the blades of a helicopter, he spun on the spot to create room. The people around them stepped back to avoid being hit by them. He spotted a gap and ploughed sideways through the crowd.

Anaïs continued to struggle but to no avail. He was too strong. With exasperation, she relented and let him carry her through the crowd. On the fringe of the crowd their way was blocked by a high fence. The Inquisitor glanced both ways down the fence line. He cursed, made a snap decision and headed in the direction of the amphitheatre.

Within moments he reached the opening. The line of uniformed personnel she had seen earlier was barring the entrance. They seemed to be filtering and sorting the crowd.

He barged through them yelling hysterically about a sick child. Anaïs grinned to herself. *You make a good actor.* Too occupied with the number of people they were dealing with, the guards put up no resistance.

Inside, he stopped and cast an eye around the amphitheatre.

'You can put me down now,' said Anaïs.

He shook his head. 'No, not until we're out of here.'

He pushed his way through the crowd to the perimeter of the arena. Mounting the stairs two at a time he rushed to the top. Anaïs was taken aback by his energy. *Man! I could use some of this.*

He paused at the pinnacle of the tiered seating, assessing his next move. Anaïs glanced down into the arena. Separated by a circle of security personnel close to the entrance was a group of figures. She peered closely at them. The bodies of a number of them were flickering, almost like fluorescent tubes which were unable to fully ignite.

'The shades,' muttered Anaïs.

The Inquisitor followed her gaze and nodded. He stepped up onto the upper edge of the amphitheatre. Anaïs joined him in looking down at the drop before them. The ground was several metres below under the canopy of a line of trees.

'Um … no. Don't even think about it,' said Anaïs.

Iggy puffed his cheeks. 'Thinking never got me anywhere, Anaïs. You either do it. Or you don't. I choose to act.' He drew in a deep breath, set his jaw and jumped.

Anaïs screwed her eyes shut and screamed out a long high-pitched 'no'. It only stopped when, upon hitting the ground, the Inquisitor squeezed her so tight it knocked the wind out of her.

DOUBT

The Inquisitor hit the ground with such force his legs buckled under him. He cushioned the impact by crumpling into a ball and rolling across the soft sand at the base of the wall. Panting, he came to rest on his back with Anaïs on top of him.

Rolling onto one side he opened his arms and released the witch from his grasp. She untangled herself and pushed away from him. They both climbed to their feet. He tilted his head and arched backwards, massaging the base of his spine. He straightened, stuck his little finger in one ear and jiggled it. Sighing, he said, 'Did you really have to do that?'

'What?' squeaked Anaïs, still trying to catch her breath after having it squeezed out of her.

'Scream in my ear.'

Anaïs set her hands on her hips and twisted her lips. 'Don't go jumping down off high walls again and you won't have that problem.'

'There wasn't a problem,' he said as he extracted

one boot at a time out of the ankle-deep sand they stood in. 'You worry too much.'

'A healthy dose of worry is a good thing,' Anaïs replied. 'It hasn't failed me in the past. Thanks for getting me out of there, though.' She turned to leave. 'I'll be off then.'

He reached out and grabbed her by the elbow. 'Wait.'

'Wait for what?' She wrenched her arm free, turning it against his thumb. 'And don't you dare touch me again.'

'Fine! I won't. But I need to talk to you.'

Anaïs curled her lip. 'I don't care what you have to say and I don't need your help.'

'You just did.'

She pulled a face indicating reluctant agreement. 'Okay, besides that.'

'It's important.'

'What is?'

'What I have to say.'

She exhaled with a puff. 'Well, spit it out then,' said Anaïs, sensing that he would give her no respite until he had said his piece.

'I'm not your enemy, Anaïs,' said Iggy with slow deliberation. 'My parents are.'

'I already gathered that about them. Although, I doubt the enemy part about you.'

'I've come to realise what they're doing is wrong. I want to apologise for my actions.'

'Yeah, right!' snapped Anaïs. 'Like I should believe

that! You've never been apologetic about anything before.'

'I'm trying to be honest here.' In frustration he wiped his brow with the back of his hand. 'You're making this very difficult.'

'Put yourself in my shoes.' Anaïs set her knuckles on her hips. 'How would you feel? You took your own sister and used her against me.'

'I know that now,' he said with genuine sorrow. 'But I didn't then. My father lied to me.'

'They lied to all of us.'

He sighed. 'Unfortunately, I now know that to be true.'

'How could you be so blind?'

'No real excuses, I'm afraid.'

His tone seemed more defensive than apologetic. It irked Anaïs. 'That's not good enough.'

'I know,' he said softly. 'I was following orders. It's what I've been trained to do. But that all changed. I realised what was really going on. That I have made a mistake. I now know what I've done is wrong. I'm here to try to make amends.'

She cast a disdainful eye over him. 'I don't trust you.'

'I fully understand. I wouldn't either. I'm only asking you to give me the benefit of the doubt.'

Unconvinced, Anaïs shook her head. 'Way too many doubts.'

'I can't make you do anything against your will, Anaïs. If you want to, you're free to go. But if you stay I can protect you. I know how they function. I know what they're capable of.'

'I've experienced that myself.' Anaïs stared at her boots. 'Given the opportunity, I know they will work against me.' She lifted her head and looked him in the eye. 'However, I don't see that you can help me any more than I can help myself.'

'They will communicate with me,' said Iggy. 'They don't know I'm with you. My orders were to find you and keep my distance. To keep an eye on you.' Furtively, he glanced around the clearing they stood in. 'We will know ahead of time what their plans are. We will be one step ahead.'

Anaïs tilted her head back. She eyed the spot where they had jumped from the top of the stadium wall. 'I think we already know more than they do.'

'Don't be too sure,' he said warily. 'They will know about this situation. Although the shades are a considerable problem for them, you are the real problem. You are a loose cannon. Believe me, if they weren't otherwise occupied they would stop at nothing to get you.'

'I know that. They already tried.'

The Inquisitor squatted in order to look Anaïs square in the eye. She averted her gaze, avoiding his penetrating stare. He laid a hand on her shoulder.

She brushed it away with the back of her hand. 'Don't touch me, I said!'

'My bad,' he said repentantly. He brought his hands together and knotted his fingers. He jabbed towards her with his thumbs. 'Listen. We are the future, Anaïs. Their ways are antiquated. They know this, but fear change. Because of this you are their greatest threat.'

'How can I possibly be a threat?' She ran the backs of her hands down her jacket and spread her arms. 'Look at me.'

'Size is immaterial, Anaïs. It's what you're capable of doing.'

Anaïs grinned. 'Well, I know I'm capable of being a pain in the posterior.'

He smiled. 'That you are. But you can do so much more than that.'

Anaïs considered his words. They reminded her of the conversation with Lilith. She had said practically the same things he was saying. But was he to be trusted?

'I need a moment,' said Anaïs.

'Certainly.'

She shooed him away. 'Go stand over there.'

He frowned. 'Why?'

'Just do it if you want me to stick around.'

He looked at her dubiously.

Folding her arms and tapping her foot in the soft sand, she waited for him to respond.

He breathed deeply though his nostrils. 'Fine!' He stood, spun on one heel and waded through the sand to a nearby rock. He sat on it and watched her.

Anaïs glared at him. He dropped his eyes and she turned her back to him. She held her arms out, brought her hands together and opened her palms. 'Sappho? Can you come here?' The ladybird released her hold on Anaïs. She crawled up her back and over her shoulder. After walking down her arm, Sappho settled on the witch's hands.

Anaïs looked over her shoulder at the Inquisitor. He

was busy removing his boots. She smirked. *Phew! Glad I'm not there to smell them.* He began to empty the sand out of them. She returned her focus to Sappho, noting with delight that the elytra had fully healed.

'Lilith?' she whispered. 'Are you there?'

The spots on Sappho's elytra swirled around and morphed into the face of the Oracle.

'Yes, Anaïs?'

'Is he to be trusted?'

'I told you before, Anaïs. Search yourself. Therein lies the answer.'

Slightly distressed, Anaïs knotted her brow. 'He talked about the same things you did.'

The eye on Sappho's back winked at her. *'Then you have your answer.'*

'But he has done terrible things.'

'Many do in the pursuit of their cause—of what they think is right.' A shadow flickered across Lilith's face. *'One man's horror is another man's solution.'*

'Scary principle.'

'It is the way of the universe.'

Anaïs dropped her eyes. She looked past Sappho at the ground between her feet. 'I have a lot of doubts.' She began to draw a circle in the sand with the toe of her boot.

'We all do,' said Lilith. *'Life is full of them. As you grow you will learn to read your instincts better. The only way to hone this skill is with practice.'*

'But that involves risk.'

'When is there ever no element of risk, Anaïs?'

Anaïs shrugged. The grin on Lilith's face drew her

attention back to the ladybird cupped in her palms. 'Never, I guess.'

'I believe in you, Anaïs. You will know what to do.'

Anaïs cracked a weak smile. 'Thanks, Lilith. I hope I can find it.'

AN ACCOMPLICE

Iggy knocked the heel of his boot against the rock to extract the last grains of sand. He looked up as Anaïs approached him. He eyed her cautiously. 'So? Are we good to go?'

'You don't mess around, do you?'

'No, of course not. Time is precious.' He pulled on his boot with a grunt. 'Like I said before, you either do something or you don't. No messing around.'

She frowned. 'I don't mess around.'

'You could have fooled me.' He indicated the ladybird on her back. 'Who in their right mind talks to their backpack?'

'It's not a back—' Anaïs stopped herself, realising the less he knew about her magic the better. Given the uncertainty of his word, she had to retain every advantage she had. If necessary, Sappho could be her key to escape.

'Oh, I do that all the time!' she exclaimed cheerfully.

He shook his head in bemusement. 'Okay,' he

murmured. 'Perhaps you can keep your idiosyncrasies to yourself.'

'I'll try to keep that in mind.'

'Good.' He studied her face for a moment. 'Shall we go?'

'Where?'

'I assume you need to find your friends.'

She pursed her lips. 'Yes, I do. But if I let you help me, what kind of guarantee do I have that you won't reveal me or them to your mother and father?'

He furrowed his brow. 'I don't know if there is anything I can give as a guarantee. I told you before, you'll have to trust me.'

Unmoved, Anaïs folded her arms. 'That's not enough for me.'

The Inquisitor cast his eyes to the sky in frustration. He shoved his hands into his coat pockets. His eyes widened. 'Hold on!'

'What?'

'I have something.'

Anaïs raised an eyebrow. 'Really?'

'Yes.' He pulled his hands out of his pockets. In one of them he held a short section of chain.

'This,' he said.

The sight of the chain cut Anaïs's breath short.

'It's for hellhounds. Without it I can't retrieve them.' He held out his hand, offering her the chain. 'This should be guarantee enough.'

She stared at the chain. Constructed from highly polished silver, its links glinted as they caught the sun. The chain was pristine. It looked as if it had never been used. Tentatively, half expecting some kind of magical surge from it, she reached out and took it. There was none. Although short in length, its weight was considerable.

She pulled off her beret. 'Heavy,' she said, as she deposited the chain into the hat. The chain disappeared into the void, and with it went its mass. She rubbed the brim of the beret, silently thanking it for taking the weight off her hands.

'I know,' said Iggy.

She held out her empty hand. Curling her fingers towards her palm, Anaïs gestured for more. Deadpan, she said, 'And the other one.'

'Other one?' he replied innocently.

Anaïs remained insistent. 'I know you have two.'

'It's the only magic I have!' he protested.

'I don't believe that. And, unless you can do anything other than retrieve hellhounds with the chains, you won't need them.'

He paused. For the first time in her experience with him, she read apprehension on his face. On the face of someone always so self-assured, it was an alien expression. It gave her confidence.

'C'mon.' Anaïs smiled slyly. 'Trust me.'

With some uncertainty he reached into his coat pocket and extracted the other chain. He hesitated. Begrudgingly, he relented and handed her the chain.

'If we need them, you'll get them back,' she reassured him as she dropped it into the beret.

Anaïs breathed easily. Not only had the physical burden of the chains been removed, but also a psychological weight had been lifted from her shoulders. She took her time replacing the beret on her head, watching him wallow in his own misgivings about what he had done.

Anaïs snorted with satisfaction. She now had control. *How the tables have turned.* She reached into her pocket and pulled out her promptuary. 'Right! Let's see where they've got to.'

She opened the handbook and instructed it to show her the location of the Catamarine. A series of light beams shot from a single point on its open page. They fanned out like searchlights before splicing together and forming a single holographic image of Athens and its surrounding islands.

The Inquisitor's jaw dropped. 'How did it do that?'

Anaïs shrugged. 'Dunno. It started doing stuff like this by itself. Pretty cool, eh?'

Iggy nodded and then shook his head in amazement. 'I'm gonna need to get me one of those.'

'You already have one. Maybe you can get it upgraded?'

He frowned. 'Upgrade? We can get upgrades?'

'Some of us get them automatically,' she said nonchalantly, jibing him.

'Okay,' he said, staring in disbelief at the image floating above the book. 'But clearly only some of us.'

'Then maybe it's a good thing you stick with me.' She nudged him in the ribs with her elbow. 'Some of my magic might rub off on you.'

He reassessed the image floating above the book. It

slowly began to rotate. 'I hope so,' he muttered to himself with a tinge of jealousy.

Anaïs scrutinised the map. At first she could not spot anything indicating the location of the Catamarine. Apprehensively, she searched the map before sighing with relief. She pointed at a small flashing dot. 'Ah! There they are.'

She commanded the promptuary to zoom in. The handbook did as requested. Near Athens, and not far off the foot of the Greek mainland, was a long, slender island. The dot appeared to be moving up its eastern coastline.

'Excellent! Now, next problem: how to get there.'

'I have a solution,' said Iggy.

Anaïs grinned. 'You sound just like someone I know.'

Thank you for taking the time to read *A Witch's Calling*.

All authors appreciate knowing what you think about their work. Posting a review and other feedback helps improve their writing, assists readers in discovering their work, and is generally accepted as good karma.

Please consider **posting an honest review** on the (web) store where you purchased this book, or on Goodreads.

Word of mouth is an author's best friend, and much appreciated.

Anaïs's adventures continue in

Magic Awakes: Anaïs Blue Book Five

The universe is out of kilter. Only Anaïs Blue can restore order.

But how is a witch supposed to do that?

The line between friend and foe is no longer clear. Nor are the borders dividing the natural and supernatural. Shades have taken control of their own lot, and the laws that keep the universe in harmony are gone.

Without her usual accomplices, who should a witch trust?

Burdened with a dark, dangerous and seemingly impossible task, Anaïs must find her way.

Will the magic she possesses be enough?

And does Anaïs have the strength to complete the task assigned to her? Especially when the solution may not be something she is prepared to face.

All will be revealed in this final instalment of the Anaïs Blue series.

Strap in. It will be quite a ride.

Hardcover ISBN: 9789492523310

ALSO BY P J WHITTLESEA

One man. No future. A rich heritage.

Indigenous urbanite Billy knows very little about his ancestry. He is quite content to let it stay that way. One late night out changes all that.

Stranded on a central Australian highway with only the stars and mosquitoes for company, he finds his future determined by a pair of unlikely saviours. And a mysterious supernatural entity.

In an effort to get home Billy embarks on a surreal odyssey. Not only into his heritage, but also into himself.

Tap here to read his remarkable story.

ISBN: 9789492523006

ABOUT THE AUTHOR

P. J. Whittlesea is an author and singer-songwriter. Originally from Australia, he now resides in Amsterdam in The Netherlands.

To find out about new releases, promotions, special sneak peaks, and to follow his writer's journey, sign up to the author's **book club**.

Scan the QR code below for access.

As a special introduction you will receive a free digital copy of:
The City of Shades: Anaïs Blue Prequel.

Ingram Content Group UK Ltd.
Milton Keynes UK
UKHW012039060623
422990UK00003B/31

9 789492 523280